Publisher: Valentina Antonia, LLC.

No Escape is the 4th book and 4th installment of an ongoing serial. For maximum enjoyment, it is recommended the serial be read in order:

No Escape

TREK MI Q'AN: BOOK 4

By Jaid Black

Prologue I

Airspace within the Kyyto Sectors, Planet Tryston

Trek Mi Q'an Galaxy, Seventh Dimension

6044 Y.Y. (Yessat Years)

She had nigh unto given up hope of ever escaping him.

Already four years had gone by—four incredibly long years since the moon-rising of her eighteenth Yessat year when her ownership had been transferred from her sire to Cam K'al Ra.

She had been given several opportunities to escape him since she'd turned eighteen, yet nothing had come of any of them. Leastways, she had made a pact with her cousins. They had made vows unto the others that 'twould be all of them who would flee together or all of them who would stay behind and remain prisoners to the fates. The closer she had gotten to the moon-rising of the claiming, the more Kara had sometimes wished she'd made no such vow. But a vow was a vow and she had given hers freely.

It had turned out to be the right decision. She had kept her oath and now the three of them would be free the soonest, together for all time.

From the moon-rising her cousin Dari had been forcibly carted off to Arak and onward, Kara Q'ana Tal had made certain to always give the appearance of being all things demure and submissive. She had given Cam K'al Ra no reason to doubt her acceptance of their impending joining and because of that fact he had been lenient toward her o'er the Yessat years, allowing her to remain in her family home with minimal guarding. He had come visiting upon occasion, kissing and licking at her body as though he'd never get enough of her, but for the most part he had left her alone, confident in her obedience.

'Twas paying off.

Kara had no desire to hurt Cam—truly she didn't. And truth be told, she felt more than a little guilty turning her back on him that she might be free.

But freedom. She shivered under the rouge-colored *vesha* hide wrapped about her. 'Twas a heady thing, a state of being Trystonni females took for granted they would get to experience after their twenty-fifth Yessat year. And yet that very thing, the rite of passage into Trystonni womanhood so many thought nothing of for 'twas considered a given, she and her cousin Dari had been systematically denied.

Nay, Kara hadn't the desire to hurt Cam, yet she hadn't the desire to succumb to his wishes either. What's more, she had matured enough through the years to realize that if she were to flee from him, she could never again return to him. Like as not, his pride would be sorely wounded and he would seek to punish her in ways she couldn't begin to imagine— terrifying, whispered about under one's breath ways that she had overheard her sire tell her *mani* about.

Kara sighed. Had she thought Cam might give her no more than a small punishment she might have considered returning to Tryston and to him after a time. But nay, he had changed too much o'er the passage of time, had become grimmer and more formidable with the advent of each new moon-rising. 'Twas for a certainty she'd be doled out the most horrific and final of punishments were she to return to him after fleeing.

The older Cam grew, the fiercer he had become. Kara had watched with much trepidation as the young, carefree hunter she had known since her youth had grown into an unbending, ruthless warlord. From untitled hunter to high lordship, from high lordship to lesser king, from lesser king to king of planet Zideon, each rise he had taken up the political ladder had come at a price. And the price he had paid in battling and bloodshed had created a formidable, domineering warrior she had no desire to be bound to.

He frightened her. Kara hated admitting as much for o'er the Yessat years she too had come into her own, had grown into a strong woman unafraid of most things. And yet there it was. Fear. Fear the likes of which she'd never before known.

"We will be free and clear of Kyyto airspace the soonest." Princess Jana Q'ana Tal whispered the words to Kara as she navigated the stolen high-speed conveyance through the shimmering gold twilight.

Kara closed her eyes briefly and sighed. "Praise the goddess. If Uncle were to catch us within his own sectors, 'twould be spankings for the deuce of us, twenty-two Yessat years apiece or no." She kept her voice lowered, as did Jana. It was as if both of them feared he'd hear them, regardless of the fact that they had almost breached the Trystonni atmosphere altogether.

Jana thought of their uncle Kil and swallowed a bit roughly. "Yet further proof that we have made the correct decision." Her nostrils flared. "Leastways, we shan't be spanked on Galis."

Kara smiled at that. "I shall still miss him," she said softly.

"Aye." Jana's eyes gentled, though she didn't turn her head from her navigating duty. "So shall I."

Kara's eyes flicked o'er her cousin. "'Tis fortunate indeed your sire permitted you to learn how to navigate a conveyance." She looked away, glancing out the wide front porthole as they breached outer space. "My sire would permit me nowhere near one."

"Mayhap he expects you to flee. Mine believes I've no reason to do so." Jana's lips curved downward into a grim smile. "In truth he would have permitted me to learn even if I'd had a reason to flee."

Kara patted her knee sympathetically. "Uncle Dak has not been the same these four Yessat years Dari has been removed to Arak."

Jana's spine went rigid. "Neither has my *mani*," she gritted out. She was silent a long moment, then said, "Leastways, I feel that by removing Dari from her prison, I am evening the score on my parents behalf a wee bit."

Kara nodded. Her eyes narrowed in thought. "I dislike the notion of bringing you bad thoughts, cousin, yet am I worried for Dari. The holo-call she sent out was nigh unto chilling..." Her voice trailed off. "My apologies," she murmured. "'Twas not necessary to say —"

"Nay." Jana's jaw went rigid. "But mark my words as truth, Kara. If Gio has beaten her, 'twill be the last action he ever makes without consequence."

Kara agreed. She couldn't begin to imagine what else could have possibly upset Dari enough to be frightened to the point of tears. 'Twasn't like Dari to have tears in her eyes at all, for she tended toward the stoic for a certainty. The best Kara and Jana could figure was that she was being maltreated — yet further proof 'twas past the time to flee.

Quiet fell between the cousins, giving Kara time to think. 'Twas something she didn't desire to do much of these days for when she did it inevitably meant that her thoughts would turn to her betrothed, or her former betrothed as it were.

Cam was going to be furious when he found out, more angered than she felt comfortable thinking on. He'd be furious at her for fleeing, at himself for being fooled by her displays of obedience, and at her *mani* and sire for not keeping a close enough vigil regarding her whereabouts. Aye — he'd be angered with them all.

Kara could live with knowing of his fury, however. 'Twas not his fury she'd be thinking about for she would be forever removed from him and any punishments he might think to inflict upon her.

She sighed. 'Twas not Cam's inevitable anger that made her flinch when she thought on him—'twas the possible hurt and embarrassment she might cause him by fleeing. She would that it could be otherwise, yet the course had been set and there was no turning back. But then, neither did she wish to turn back.

Freedom. Her sire and betrothed had tried to deny her, but she would not be denied. Daughter of the Emperor or no, she would be no warrior's battle prize.

"We've reached the shield," Jana murmured.

Kara's head shot up. Her hearts rate began to accelerate, knowing as she did that all of their planning came down to this one moment in time. If the codes she had stolen from the warring chamber were accurate, their ship would be permitted to breach the invisible energy field her sire had ordered commissioned only three Yessat years past to guard the planet. But if the codes were wrong...

"Let us pray to Aparna that our ship is not instantly disintegrated." Kara took a deep breath then looked at her cousin. "Are you ready for the codes?"

Jana did a little deep breathing of her own. Moisture gathered between her breasts and on her brow as an acute sense of fear settled into the pit of her stomach. "Aye," she whispered hoarsely. "Read them to me."

Kara closed her eyes briefly and sent up one last prayer to the goddess. Clutching the *trelli* parchment firmly in both hands, she opened her eyes and began reading off the hieroglyphic-like symbols that corresponded to Trystonni numbers. "*Sii, Sii, Fala, Sii...*" She continued to read off the numbers in a slow, measured tone until the last one had been keyed in by Jana.

"'Tis done," Jana said quietly.

Kara nodded, her breath coming out in a rush. "'Twill take but mere seconds." She sucked in a lungful of air and unconsciously held it. Her eyes wide, she grabbed her cousin's hand and squeezed it as the deuce of them awaited their shared fate together. 'Twould be death or freedom.

As their ship thrust through the Trystonni energy field, they both released a pent-up breath, grinning as they hugged each other. "We did it!" Kara beamed. "We well and truly did it!"

Jana smiled fully as she switched on the dimmer control. The dimmer allowed the high-speed conveyance to become invisible to detection scanners, but it also made her job as navigator more difficult. Leastways, passing-by conveyances and other assorted ships wouldn't be able to see their craft to know to steer clear of it. 'Twould take much concentration to navigate the conveyance to Arak.

"Aye." Jana chuckled. "'Tis nigh unto impossible to believe, but we are free and clear of Trystonni airspace."

"How many Nuba hours to Arak?"

"Approximately five."

Kara nodded. "I shall remain quiet so as not to distract you."

The next few hours proved to be the longest of Kara's life. Nearing Arak also meant nearing the chance that the three of them would be caught and punished accordingly. She couldn't begin to imagine how horrific their punishments would be, but she knew they'd be harsh for a certainty.

There were approximately six hours left of the moon-rising, six hours until the dominant sun broached the Tryston sky and declared it morn. Her absence would be noticed mayhap an hour or two after that. That gave them seven Nuba hours at worst and eight Nuba hours at best to snatch Dari away and hightail it to Galis. There was no time for mistakes.

A horn-like sound blared just then, breaking both escaped princesses out of their quiet reverie. Kara's gaze shot toward the communicator. Her eyes rounded. "'Tis another holo-call from Dari," she muttered.

Jana's brow furrowed. Why would her sister be calling an hour before they were scheduled to dock? "A recorded message or a living dimensional representation?"

Kara's fingers flicked o'er the complex keyboard. She punched in directives until the requisite information appeared on screen. "'Twas recorded two Nuba minutes past and 'tis labeled as urgent." She keyed in another sequence, commanding the communicator to play the recorded memory. "'Twill take a few seconds for it to rewind and play—ahh here we go."

A moment later, Princess Dari's three-dimensional image appeared on a display screen that emerged from the front ceiling of the conveyance. She looked frightened, Kara thought nervously. Something had spooked her for a certainty.

Greetings unto you, sister and cousin. I fear I haven't much time to speak, so this message will be brief...

Dari looked o'er her shoulder, quickly ascertaining that she hadn't been followed. She turned back around to face the recorder, throwing three long micro-braids o'er her shoulder as she did so. Her almond-shaped eyes were wildly rounded, the fear in their glowing blue depths apparent.

Head for Galis with all speed, she choked out. *Do not come here to aid me for I cannot leave. Not yet.*

Horrified, Kara glanced at Jana with her mouth agape. She couldn't begin to imagine why Dari would want them to leave her behind. Leastways, it made no sense. Dari hated—

An evil dwells here, Dari murmured. *An evil that must be destroyed.* She swallowed shakily, closing her eyes briefly. *I mayhap have not the power to destroy it myself, yet I will not leave Arak until I've enough information to —*

The sound of approaching footsteps caused Dari to stop speaking and turn on her heel to gage who it was that was about to come upon her. She turned back to the recorder and spoke quickly.

I must go. Vow it to me that the deuce of you will not return to Tryston. Forge onward to Galis and create your new destinies. I will join you the soonest. 'Tis a vow amongst cousins, she adamantly swore.

Dari then hesitated, mayhap deciding how much time she had left to speak. In the end she decided to risk another Nuba second's worth of speech.

Worry not o'er me, for I will be passing fair. The Evil One knows not that I am aware of its existence. Please, she begged, *do not return to your impending matrimonial prisons. I will join you the soonest,* she whispered fervently. *I have figured out how to escape —*

The holo-call abruptly ended, leaving Kara and Jana more than a little frightened for Dari's safety. They turned to look at each other, both of their expressions horrified. 'Twasn't necessary to speak, for both of them implicitly understood what the other one was thinking.

What evil one had Dari spoken of? Why had the recording ended so abruptly — had Dari been caught or had she merely switched off the holo-recorder device herself? Should they risk returning to Tryston and mayhap get caught in the doing to inform their sires of Dari's predicament, or should they continue onward as Dari had directed them to do? Would she truly be able to escape without aid?

"What do we do?" Jana whispered. She sounded lost. Frightened and lost.

Kara nibbled on her lower lip as her fingers danced once again o'er the main communicator's keyboard. "First things first, cousin. I must ascertain whether 'twas Dari who ended that holo-call or if 'twas an unexpected interloper who ended it for her."

Jana nodded as she steered the conveyance away from Arak and toward Galis. "If the genetic map of any but Dari shows up on the fingerprint scan, we must turn ourselves in for a certainty that we might inform our sires of what we know."

"Agreed." Kara pulled up the recorded memory and punched in a sequence of keystrokes. She waited what felt like forever for the communicator to analyze the fingerprint scan. When 'twas done, she turned to Jana. "Dari ended it," she murmured. "'Twas her genetic map and no other's."

Jana blew out a breath of relief. "Thank the goddess."

"Aye."

They sat there in silence for a suspended moment, both of them realizing they had little time to make a decision. Their sires would send out hunting calls the soonest. If they chose to continue onward to Galis as Dari had instructed them to do, 'twas now or never to see it through.

Now or never, Kara thought anxiously. They had to breach Galis airspace before every hunter in Trek Mi Q'an was alerted to their escape.

Jana swallowed a bit roughly before she spoke. Her voice came out in a shaky whisper. "I vote we carry onward."

Kara's eyes widened. "But what of D—"

"In my hearts," Jana said adamantly, "I know my sister will make good on her word. I know this for a certainty."

Kara said nothing to that. 'Twas true that blood siblings shared a mental bond that others could not feel or understand the why of. Yet still…

"I, more so than you, have my reasons for desiring to continue on to Galis. But I will not go unless 'tis certain you are that—"

"I am," Jana said simply. "I know Dari will come to us."

Kara blew out a breath. She turned away from Jana and stared out of the front porthole of the conveyance.

"What is your final decision?" Jana asked anxiously. She was clearly too emotionally charged up to trust her own judgment on so critical a matter.

Kara pondered that question o'er for a torturous moment. 'Twas for a certainty neither Jana nor herself would know happiness again if anything happened to Dari. And yet her cousin had seemed so certain of herself, so convinced that she could escape Arak and join them on Galis...

"We will continue onward," Kara said quietly. Her glowing blue gaze tracked the movement of a passing meteorite that Jana's navigating had expertly dodged. "And we will pray to the goddess 'tis the right decision."

Prologue II

Palace of the Dunes

Sand City on planet Tryston

Fourteen Nuba hours later

Cam K'al Ra, the King of planet Zideon, strode through the great hall with all haste. His harsh features grew all the grimmer when he took notice of the weeping *manis* seated at the raised table offering each other solace. The High King Jor was seated between them, his large palms stroking both his mother and auntie's backs.

This, Cam conceded, did not bode well. He hadn't the faintest notion why he had been summoned before the Emperor, yet he was now certain that it somehow involved his betrothed. The Empress would not be weeping otherwise. He would not have been summoned otherwise.

"Ari predicted something bad would happen," Kyra choked out. She leaned against her son as though she couldn't hold herself upright without aid. "But I never thought..."

"I don't believe it," Geris said shakily, her normally authoritative voice subdued, her eyes unblinking, "my firstborn baby is gone."

Cam's entire body stilled. The breath went out of him at the Queen's words. He stopped in his tracks and slowly turned on his boot heel to face the family that would one day soon be his own.

Jana was gone? he thought warily. That could only mean that—

14

"We'll find them," sixteen-year-old Jor murmured. "Already the finest hunters of Tryston are scouting for the conveyance."

Them, Cam thought as his hearts rate sped up, his future brother-within-the-law had used the word *them*.

Wasting no more time, Cam made an abrupt about-face and strode briskly toward the warring chamber. Something had happened to Kara, he told himself as his mind raced with the possibilities. Something bad. Mayhap she had even been kidnapped. His nostrils flared in protest as he considered what would happen to his betrothed if she had been captured by insurrectionists, what would become of her if they —

Nay. He could not allow himself to think on it. 'Twas sorely apparent he would need his wits about him to find her.

When he entered the warring chamber, Cam knew for a certainty that his assumption had been correct. Every of the Q'an Tal warriors was present, the four ruling brothers gathered around the planning table with their commanding captains at their sides.

Kara was gone.

Cam could see it in their expressions as they noticed his entrance and looked up at him from their seats. He could see it in the bloodshot eyes of the Emperor and King Dak as they stared at him with troubled expressions. They had both lost daughters today.

But, he thought with a sudden flash of premonition, there was something more to this...

As Cam's eyes flicked about the warring chamber, he noticed for the first time that some of the warriors within it were throwing him pitying glances. Kil's gaze shifted from Cam's eyes and looked away as if he felt...embarrassed.

But that made no sense. Why would the King of Morak be embarrassed for him? And then Cam noticed yet the same shifting of eyes from King Rem. Rem's face flushed slightly before he too looked away from him.

Something was wrong — something was very wrong.

"Just tell me," Cam said hoarsely, the muscles in his heavy body cording. He felt the eyes of every warrior in the chamber turn to him as he spoke. "What has become of Kara?"

Throats cleared. Eyes darted away. Warriors shifted uncomfortably upon their seats.

Cam's nostrils flared. In that moment he knew for a certainty that his betrothed had not been kidnapped. But nay, he thought angrily, if she had not been kidnapped then that could only mean that she had —

"'Tis sorry I am," Zor muttered as he met Cam's gaze.

His hands fisted at his sides, inducing the veins on his forearms to bulge. "Just tell me," Cam gritted out. He cared not that his tone of voice bordered on impudence. "Tell me what has happened."

But he already knew, of course. He just wanted to hear the words aloud, needed his worst fears confirmed.

"She is gone," Zor said softly. "Kara and Jana have fled Tryston together."

Cam stood there rooted to the ground for what felt to be an hour. His breathing was labored — labored in the way all warriors' breathing becomes when they are in a temper with their wenches yet trying to control it. His nostrils continued to flare with each heaving of angered breath he took. His hands fisted and unfisted at his sides as he allowed the impact of the Emperor's words to sink in.

She was gone. Kara had run away from him.

Cam's head shot up. He narrowed his glowing blue-green eyes at the warriors looking upon him with pity. "I will find her," he growled. His heated gaze found Zor. "And when I do 'tis my right to remove her from her birth home since 'tis obvious she has not been watched o'er properly here."

Zor's nostrils flared at the words that had been hissed at him like venom. "I watched o'er her well," he ground out. "'Tis not I that my hatchling fled from."

Zor's face flushed guiltily when he heard his brothers suck in their breath on Cam's behalf. He took a deep breath and expelled it. "I offer you my apologies, Cam." He stood up, looking as weary as Cam felt. "You are correct for a certainty," he rasped out. "Had I guarded her more vigilantly then—"

"Nay." Cam held up a palm, then ran it o'er his chin as his thoughts turned back to his betrothed. He sighed. "I offer you my apologies as well. We are both—we are...we are not ourselves just now."

Kil stood up and walked towards the deuce of them, his fingers intertwined with those of his three-year-old son Kilian. "We will find her. We will find both of them." When he was upon them, he drew his face closer that none but Zor and Cam might hear him. "I ask but one boon, Cam."

One of Cam's golden eyebrows arched in inquiry, but he said nothing. He was beyond words really. He was so angered that—

"Do not cause my niece a harm when you find her," Kil said under his breath to keep their conversation private. "'Tis for a certainty you feel shamed, yet I still ask that you show Kara a bit of mercy. She is but young and confused."

Cam's nostrils flared. He felt the need to attack something, to punch at someone until his fists bled. But he would never—could never—hurt Kara. "She will be spanked as is my right," he gritted out, "but nay, I shan't harm her."

Kil nodded his understanding. Had he been Cam he would have done the same.

"'Tis time to talk strategy," Dak announced from across the chamber as he motioned toward them to take their seats. "We best get on with it."

Cam was about to join him at the planning table when the sound of loud footfalls jogging towards the warring chamber snagged his attention. A Nuba-second later, High King Jor strode in briskly, his pathway veering straight towards Zor and Cam.

"What is it?" Zor bellowed to his heir. "Has word come back from any of the hunting parties?"

"Aye," Jor confirmed as he panted for air. He jogged the remaining space that separated him from his sire, coming to a halt before him and Cam. His glowing blue gaze flicked back and forth between the two warriors. "'Tis bad news," he rasped out.

Cam's entire body went deathly still. He awaited Jor's words much like one would await a sentence to the gulch pits—quiet dignity on the outside, dread on the inside. "What has happened?" he asked hoarsely. "What has become of wee Kara?"

Jor closed his eyes briefly and inhaled a calming lungful of air. His chest rose and fell with each labored breath that he took. "Kara and Jana attempted to land on Galis," he murmured as his eyes opened and bore into Cam's. "Leastways, they did not make it."

"What do you mean, son?" Zor asked softly.

Jor's gaze flicked from Cam to his sire, then back to Cam. "Their ship was disintegrated," he said roughly. "Kara and Jana are dead."

The warring chamber fell into silence. Not a word, not a sound, not even a breath could be heard.

Cam tried to control himself, tried with all of his Yessat years worth of brutal training to remain stoic—but he could not. "Nay!" he bellowed, his arm flinging wildly through the air. "They are not dead. Those hunters know nothing!"

Cam felt Kil's hand upon his shoulder, attempting to comfort him, but he shrugged it off. "Nay," he ground out. "I am not mad! Think you I would not know it in my hearts if Kara had passed through the Rah?" He backed away from Kil, from Jor, from the quietly crying Emperor. "They," he said distinctly, his teeth gritting, "are wrong."

But as Cam's eyes flicked o'er the chamber, as he took in the solemn expressions of those around him, his breathing grew more and more labored for he knew he was grasping at nothingness in a futile attempt to hold on to the only woman in existence who could complete him.

Tears came to his eyes. "Nay," Cam said softly. He continued to back away from the other warlords until a crystal wall stopped him from going further. "Nay," he rasped out.

The sound of Zor's footsteps leaving the chamber broke the quiet. Cam's eyes tracked the movement and he noticed that the Emperor was on the verge of losing any tentative control he might still have left o'er his emotions. Not wanting to shame himself in front of so many, Zor made his exit before he did.

Cam wished he had the energy to do the same. But nay. All he could do was stand there. All he could think of was—

"Kara," Cam said softly, his eyes unblinking, "why did you run from me, *pani*?"

His love for her and need of her had been an all-consuming one. So strong were his emotions where she was concerned that he had purposely stayed away these past four Yessat years, afraid as he was that he wouldn't be able to keep himself from claiming her if he didn't. Mayhap, he thought as a renegade tear slipped unchecked down his cheek, mayhap if he had spent more time in her company she would not have feared him enough to flee.

Yet now it mattered not, for she was gone. Kara was gone and she wasn't coming back.

King Cam K'al Ra fell to his knees and wept.

Chapter One

The Trefa Jungle

Approximately one Nuba-hour outside of Valor City

Planet Galis, 6049 Y.Y. (Yessat Years)

With the silent and agile cunning of a *heeka-beast* stalking its prey, Kara Gy'at Li, nee Kara Q'ana Tal, slithered on all fours atop the dense tropical forest floor of the Trefa jungle. Like the other pack hunters accompanying her today, she wore a pair of thigh-high leather maroon combat boots, but was otherwise completely naked. Her body had been smeared all o'er with maroon *tishi* paint by male servants, allowing her and the other female warriors she hunted with to blend in with the maroon jungle that surrounded them.

"Jana," Kara murmured into the communication device fastened into one ear, "I have a visual confirmation of the prey. Proceed with Operation Bag and Tag."

Ten Yessat yards away, Jana raised one fist — the Galian equivalent to the thumbs-up symbol — to the bride-to-be situated to her left. "Ready your hunters, Tora." She whispered the words under her breath whilst simultaneously clicking on her *maltoosa* to stunner mode. "Proceed on three." Her eyes narrowed in concentration as she stealthily crept under a *tu-tu* bush. "One," she murmured into the communication device shared by every pack hunter on the mission. "Two…"

Kara felt her muscles clench in anticipation, awaiting the final signal from Jana to ambush. When Jana said "three", all the hellfire in *Nukala* would break loose. A quick glance to the right confirmed that the other Gy'at Li sisters were ready to strike as well. Kari and Klykka held their *maltoosas* firmly in hand, whilst Dorra prepared her laser scan.

All was prepared.

The prey had been surrounded on all four sides.

'Twas ridiculous in the extreme to hunt humanoid males, she thought grimly.

"...Three!"

"*Banzai!*" In unison, the pack hunters roared out the battle cry that had been taught to them by Kari Gy'at Li as they exploded from the jungle on all sides and encircled the frightened Galian males. The males screamed out their terror, two of them fainting dead away on the spot at the sight of so many women warriors preparing to subdue them as marriage chattel.

The remaining two males began to slowly back away, their eyes wide with upset and their lips threatening to break into sobbing quivers.

Crying males, fainting males — Kara half sighed and half harrumphed. Her lips pinched together disapprovingly. Five Yessat years past, she had sought freedom from a certain Trystonni warrior for this? Ahh, 'twas ironic for a certainty.

"Kara!" Dorra bellowed as she sprinted away from the enclosure of males. "The big one is getting away. Aid me, sister!"

Kara's head shot up. Her glowing blue eyes narrowed at the form of the retreating male. By the sands, she grumbled, 'twas the six-and-a-half-footer hightailing it into the thick of the jungle. Males of that height and brawn were highly coveted hunting booty because they garnered such large sums from the brides who desired a marriage union with them. Leastways, that particular six-and-a-half-footer would garner them no sum at all for Dorra coveted him as a mate for herself.

"I'm right behind you." Kara wasted no time in aiding Dorra. She had spent the last five Yessat years on Galis learning to become a proficient warrior and pack hunter. 'Twas what she excelled at. 'Twas why all hunting parties desired to count her amongst their numbers. She was fast, she was agile, and she was wicked-good at bagging and tagging.

Bagging and tagging, the Galian equivalent to courtship, was a sport Kara had never dreamed existed back when she'd been a little girl on Tryston. Wenches hunting down males for mates? 'Twas unheard of on a planet where 'twas the males who did the hunting and the females who got captured.

But Galis was a different culture altogether, a fact that reared its head in just about every facet of daily life. Bagging and tagging pack-hunting parties, for instance, operated every moon-rising during the hunting season. Sometimes Kara was a part of the pack, sometimes she was not. Leastways, if the price offered by the potential bride desirous of having a particular male bagged and tagged was exorbitant enough to lure her, Jana, and the other Gy'at Li sisters into hunting, she usually was a part of it.

This particular pack hunt would reap Kara, Jana, and their adoptive sisters a large sum of credits. Having decided to kill five *haja* birds with one *trelli* stone, the Gy'at Lis had set out last moon-rising to capture four prime male specimens at the same time. One of those males, the six-and-a-half-footer, would be Dorra's mate and therefore garner them no wage, but the other three they had been contracted to hunt down by their brides-to-be would reap them nigh unto fifty thousand credits in total.

Hunting season was o'er in a fortnight, so 'twas necessary to earn as many credits as possible. With the close of hunting season, the Gy'at Lis would holiday for a month, then recommence their tutelage in the erotic arts. Leastways, now that the five of them garnered such high pack-hunting wages, 'twas no longer necessary to perform serving wench jobs at

23

dives to earn a living. Instead, their family unit devoted itself to pack-hunting, which reaped a living that was large enough to pay for all five of them to be schooled in the erotic arts.

For a Galian female, there was no greater honor than being named a High Mystik of Valor City — a title none but the most schooled in the erotic and warring arts could claim. Kara was proud of the fact that one member of her adoptive family — Klykka — was already a High Mystik. And then there was Kari — 'twould take her mayhap one more season of apprenticing before her mistress granted her with a sector of her own to rule o'er. 'Twas Klykka who ruled o'er the sector of Gy'at Li.

Kara clicked on her *zorgs* and took flight. She concentrated on recapturing the retreating male, ignoring Jana's cry-out to Kari that a six-footer was escaping. Kari could handle the six-footer without aid. 'Twas nigh unto child's play for a wench so close to becoming a High Mystik.

Flying at a high speed directly toward the six-and-a-half-footer, Kara waited until the precise moment she was upon him before aiming her *maltoosa* down and firing it. The male bellowed, making a sound of pain before stumbling to the ground and landing on his backside. Unable to move, he could do naught but watch as Kara landed before him, wearing her thigh-high maroon combat boots, and the maroon warpaint spread all o'er her naked body.

"Shh," Kara soothed as she squatted down beside him. "'Twill do you no good to get yourself all worked up." She could see his chest heaving up and down from his labored breathing, which she'd come to realize o'er the years meant that the male was both tired from the stunning and frightened of his impending fate.

The entire ritual was too close to Trystonni mating for her to have a care for. Only in this situation the roles had been reversed and 'twas the male who had been rendered nigh unto unconscious that he might not flee from his future mate.

When Kara searched the male's terrified gaze, she couldn't help but to think of her own situation — or the situation that would have been hers had she remained on Tryston.

Kara knew that although the bagged male was frightened just now, he would be happy for his fate after he joined his body with Dorra's. On the next moon-rising when Dorra claimed him for a mate, his hearts would belong to her as well as his body. 'Twas ever the way of things on Galis.

Nay — she cared not for the similarities between the Galians and the Trystonnis for it made her wonder whether or not her hearts would have swooned with love if —

Nay. 'Twas no sense in dwelling upon it. She was dead to him now.

Kara sighed, not having a care for the direction her thoughts were straying in. She shook her head as if willing them away, then absently wondered to herself how long it would take Dorra to catch up with them. The six-and-a-half-footer wasn't the only tired one. This pack hunt had lasted two straight moon-risings, the four males having escaped once before. Dorra had chosen her mate well, she conceded. The male was cunning and agile and would gift her with many strong daughters.

The captured male's breathing grew more labored, which induced Kara to break out of her contemplative thoughts. "There now," she cooed as she removed the loincloth he wore, "'tis naught to fear of your mistress Dorra." She came down on her knees beside him and leaned o'er him, that her breasts dangled before him. "She is the bravest of warriors and skilled in all things erotic. No male could be happier with a bride such as Dorra Gy'at Li."

The male's breathing began to calm, which caused Kara to smile. She grabbed his thick penis by the root and began to slowly masturbate him up and down with one hand whilst she soothingly stroked his chest with the other. 'Twas the least she could do to keep him bagged and calm until Dorra caught up with them and tagged him.

The male's eyes closed on a shaky expelling of breath. Kara could tell from his innocent, unschooled reaction to her touching that he was still a virgin—a fact that would please the future mother of his children immensely.

"Please," the male whimpered, realizing he could do naught to stop her from stroking his manpart for the stunner had zapped his energy, "I—ohh," he breathed out. His teeth gritted. "Please do not make me do bad things, mistress."

He sounded as if he were about to cry. Kara sighed. Sure enough, she espied tears welling up in his lavender eyes. His bottom lip began to tremble. "I'm not that kind of boy," he sobbed.

Kara resisted the urge to roll her eyes. Leastways, she had learned o'er the Yessat years that all Galian males were given to extreme emotion. So instead she smiled down at him, but did not cease the stroking of his cock. "What is your name?" she asked gently.

His bottom lip continued to quiver as his eyelashes batted away his tears. "Vrek," he said shakily.

"'Tis a nice name, Vrek." She smiled as her voice gentled yet further. "I think it best do you allow yourself to be a naughty boy, Vrek. 'Tis for a certainty your mistress will expect much more from you on the next moon-rising when she takes you to the *vesha* hides."

She immediately realized 'twas the wrong thing to say. The six-and-a-half-footer's eyes widened on a gasp, then ten seconds later he broke down into a fit of uncontrollable crying.

Kara winced. By the sands, what had she been thinking, scaring him as she had in regards to his wedding night? She sighed. Her only excuse was that her mind was distracted as of late. Distracted with thoughts of a warrior she had no business musing o'er. She had given him up all of those Yessat years past, and now 'twas for a certainty he would never again welcome her home with open arms.

As her adoptive sister Kari would say, hindsight is 20-20. The past could not be changed.

But she didn't care, she firmly reminded herself. She would one day be named a High Mystik of Valor City and would rule o'er a sector all her own. 'Twas what she wanted. 'Twas what she had aspired to when first she'd arrived on Galis with Jana. So why then must she keep reminding herself of her own happiness?

Because, she thought forlornly, naught had turned out the way she had envisioned it would when she'd been a young and immature twenty-two Yessat years and determined to carve out her own destiny. She hadn't truly considered the fact that she'd never again be able to go home to Tryston. Aye, she had known it in her head, but not in her hearts. She missed her family. And she hated the fact that they all thought her long dead. Her beloved sire, her equally beloved *mani*…

An image of her favored sibling Jor popped into her mind, causing her to smile sadly. Jor would be twenty-one Yessat years now — nigh close to the age when Cam Ka'l Ra had first made his claim o'er Kara's future known.

Cam, she thought with a nostalgic smile. When she had been a girl-child still clinging to her *mani's* skirt, she had loved him with all of her hearts. His tall, muscled form and golden good looks had made him seem larger than life to her. The way he'd always had a care for her, the way his glowing *matpow*-colored eyes had always promised to cherish her — mayhap 'twas possible he had coveted her as more than a marriage prize. Mayhap he had actually loved —

Cease your mental babbling, Kara! she chastised herself. *You are free. Independent and free. 'Twas what you wanted, remember?*

Kara's nostrils flared as she began masturbating Vrek in fast, firm strokes. Bah! 'Twas ridiculous, this bagging business. The males of Galis were far too weak and unschooled to have a care for.

The male began to moan loudly at the frenzied milking of his cock, replacing the weeping he had been doing but Nuba-moments prior. "Mistress," he said hoarsely as his chest heaved up and down and sweat broke out on his forehead, "please do n — *ooooh*."

Vrek closed his eyes as his entire body shuddered, then convulsed on a groan of completion. Warm liquid shot up from his cock, spewing from the hole at the thick tip and saturating his belly.

Kara grinned at the look of bliss on his face. 'Twas much the way she had felt the first time her favored *Kefa* had brought her to peak. "Now that wasn't so bad, was it?" she asked in an exaggeratedly patient tone. 'Twas said with more patience than she felt for a certainty. "'Twill feel even better when your mistress impales her channel upon your cock and rides you into spurting within her."

Vrek's eyes rounded. "'Twill feel better?" he whispered.

"Aye." Kara smiled, making the pep talk up as she went along. In truth, she had no notion what being mounted felt like for she was still a virgin herself. Try as she might, she hadn't been able to bring herself to couple with the male servants as other Galian wenches were wont to do. "'Twill feel like bliss."

Her adoptive sister Kari had told her that the inability to couple with the servants was an affliction brought on by having dabbled with a warrior. Leastways, 'twas the very affliction Kari had suffered from ever since she'd been mounted by a warrior nine Yessat years past. Kari had coupled with no one since she'd fled from the warrior — the same as Kara had been unable to couple at all.

28

Vrek's breathing calmed as he considered that. "For a certainty?" he squeaked.

Kara nodded her head. "Aye."

Just then Dorra burst through the maroon jungle trees, the severe look of the huntress making her features appear grim. 'Twas a sight that sent Vrek's eyes back into tearing fits. Kara grunted, her lips puckering into a frown as she rose to greet her sister. "I had him calmed, dunce. Look what you've gone and done."

Dorra grunted back, her severe look softening when she laid eyes upon her hunting booty. Naked but for her thigh-high maroon boots and the warpaint she was sporting, her breasts bobbed up and down as she strode briskly toward the six-and-a-half-footer and prepared to tag him. Her nipples hardened into tight points as she came down beside him and ran a hand along the sleek contours of his body. For a male who was not a warrior, Kara had to admit he was impressive of face and form. She knew for a certainty why Dorra coveted him so.

"Calm thyself," Dorra murmured as she gently swiped away his tears with a thumb. "'Tis naught to fear of me, handsome one."

She placed the laser scan across the length of his cock and detonated it. The highly advanced chemical branding device made a whirring sound, then a moment later Vrek was officially tagged. 'Twas done. The six-and-a-half-footer could never couple with any wench but Dorra or his cock would explode.

When Vrek whimpered, Dorra soothed the stinging sensation the laser scan had left behind by running her tongue across the length of the brand. "'Twill be all healed in time for me to claim you next moon-rising," she murmured between licks. "From the morrow onward, thy body will know naught but sweet bliss from mine."

As she watched the Galian claiming scene unfold, Kara idly considered the fact that a warrior would never submit to being tagged. A warrior would have done his own brand of tagging via a bridal necklace. When the noise of hysterically sobbing Galian males reached her ears through the dense Trefa jungle, she wondered if that would have been such a bad thing.

Kara grimaced at the inferior sound. Trystonni females might grow frightened when they are claimed by warriors, but the wenches are never so weak-willed as to succumb to tearing fits. She sighed, realizing as she did that she had better grow accustomed to Galian males and their inferior temperaments the soonest.

She had no choice. 'Twas either that or never be mated.

Kara gritted her teeth. 'Twas ironic for a certainty.

Chapter Two

Holo-Port 3

Trader City, Planet Arak

Trek Mi Q'an Galaxy

Dari Q'ana Tal released a pent-up breath of air when she felt the gastrolight cruiser lurch upwards and broach the Arakian atmosphere. From her hiding place within Pod Nine, she quickly calmed herself, carefully ensuring that she made not even the smallest of sounds. She would do naught to give herself away. Even her eyes were kept closed that her glowing blue orbs might not give so much as a hint that a stowaway was aboard ship.

Dari clutched tightly the hand of the boy-child she had rescued, letting him know without words that all would be well. She could feel Bazi shaking beside her, not a surprising reaction for a child who had seen but nine Yessat years.

In truth, she was a bit wary of their predicament. She knew that if their hiding place was discovered they would be sent back to Arak in all haste.

Dari shivered. Neither she nor Bazi could ever go back, for the Evil One now knew that she was aware of its existence. It would have killed her and Bazi had she not fled the palace in all haste. Mayhap it would even have killed Gio when he discovered how and why she had died…

Gio, she thought on a pang of emotion. She had tried to remain steadfast, had attempted to thwart him at every turn o'er the past nine Yessat years, yet he had managed to do the unthinkable: he had gotten under her skin and into her hearts.

Yet she could not return to him. There were reasons. Reasons he would never forgive her for.

Leastways, that was a separate story.

Chapter Three

Kopa'Ty Palace

Planet Zideon, Trek Mi Q'an Galaxy

Panting for air, King Cam K'al Ra emerged naked from the lulling silver waters of Loch Lia-Rah, his darkly bronzed skin glistening of dew droplets, his golden hair dark with wetness. This moon-rising, as he'd done every moon-rising for more Yessat years than he could remember, Cam had circumnavigated the loch four times, which kept his heavily muscled body fitter than that of most warriors. He had an endurance few could match let alone surpass.

When he had been naught but the lowly son of a credits-poor *trelli* miner, he had swum the polluted, dirty loch of his sector every moon-rising. The waters had been so dirty 'twas nigh unto impossible to see where one was swimming, yet he had done it without complaint. He had been raised amongst the ruins left behind by greedy sector lords — insurrectionists who thought naught of burning an entire village to the ground did it help them make their point and scare the people they ruled o'er into submission. Cam supposed that because he hadn't known any other way of life, he had accepted his surroundings unthinkingly, never realizing there was a better way.

One morn Cam had gone off to labor within the *trelli* mines — slave labor he now realized himself to have been — and when he returned home for the eve, 'twas only to find that his own village had been burned to the ground. Everyone that he loved — his *mani*, his ailing papa, even his wee siblings—all of them had died in the *gastro-gel* fire set ablaze by the sector's own High Lord.

Cam had gone insane—as insane as the starved gulch beasts that sometimes leave their pits in Koror to hunt humanoid flesh whenever their food supply grows too low. Like a hungered gulch beast, Cam had spent the next few Yessat months hunting down the humanoid flesh of the rebel leader who had murdered his family. He had tracked him, stalked him, waited for the right moment to make his move, and then he had killed him.

He had experienced no guilt for the High Lord had deserved his fate for a certainty. Cam had played the part of the executioner and had thought no more on it, deciding that since he had avenged his family 'twas time to move on and find work in another *trelli* mine.

He hadn't realized at the time that the High Lord was wanted by the Emperor for treason. Or that a warlord named Kil Q'an Tal had witnessed the mortal sentence he had handed down to the rebel.

Two months later, Cam had been working the mines in a sector twenty days walk from his birth village when three finely dressed warriors had entered the squabble of a place where he had found employment and had demanded to speak to him directly. The warriors had been donned in blue leathers—the emblem of High Lords—so Cam had absently wondered if they had been sent to kill him for murdering one of their own. Leastways, he would have welcomed death at the time, for 'twas all he really had to look forward to in those days. With his family dead, there had been naught in life to recommend living—and worse yet he had barely been earning enough credits at the mines to rent a cheap chamber to sleep in.

But nay, the warriors had not come to murder him. They had come instead to inform him that he had been hand-picked as one of the few select to study the warring arts under the Emperor's tutelage.

Cam could still recall the way his good friend Jek had grinned at him when Cam had hoarsely told him there must have been a mistake. Of course, Jek hadn't been his friend at the time—'twas the first time they'd ever laid eyes on the other. Cam had argued that he was but the son of a *trelli* miner—that he knew naught of the warring arts, but Jek had insisted that no mistake had been made, that the Emperor's brother and heir apparent had witnessed Cam's hunting prowess with his own eyes and wanted him trained to be on the right side of the battling.

The first time Cam had laid eyes on the Palace of the Dunes he had nigh unto swallowed his own tongue. The wealth of the stronghold had been beyond his ken. Finely dressed and highly skilled warriors were everywhere. Beautiful, topless serving wenches abounded, their lush breasts bobbing up and down as they saw to their duties. Gorgeous, enchanted *Kefa* slaves created in every hue imaginable stood passively about, doing naught else but await the attention of the master.

All of those women—enchanted and real—had belonged to one man, to the Emperor. Their channels existed to milk him, their mouths to suckle him—and Cam had admired the arrogance of the warrior able to bring so many under his dominion.

The first time he had swum the loch contained within the grounds of the Palace of the Dunes, Cam had felt a boyish giddiness move through him. He, Cam K'al Ra, son of a *trelli* miner, was living in Sand City training under the most powerful male humanoid in existence and was permitted to make use of the most elaborate and clean loch his eyes had ever beheld. That water had been as sweetly silver as the waters of the loch he now swam in—his very own.

35

But where the mirror-clear waters of the loch within the lands of the Palace of the Dunes had inspired him, Loch Lia-Rah's waters haunted him. Every moon-rising back in Sand City, Cam had stared at the reflection cast back at him from the waters before he'd jumped in and did his nightly exercise. The reflection had been one filled with promise, with hope for a new life and a better future. For the first time in ever, he had felt as though he were at last on the right track, that there was naught to look forward to but bliss.

But now, in the present he called his own, Cam had not a care for his reflection, for it held none of the promise that his man-child reflection had. He deliberately never gazed upon himself before jumping into Loch Lia-Rah, for he knew there was naught there to see but grim lines and harsh features.

In Sand City, there had been hope. On Planet Zideon, there was naught. When Kara had died, his hearts had died with her.

Cam pulled on his leathers and strode back toward the palace, and to his harem.

* * * * *

"What?" Cam's head came up as if in slow motion. He summoned a bottle of vintage *matpow* from the raised table and settled into his *vesha*-bench. "I think it best do you start from the beginning before you tell me the whole of it."

Sitting across from Cam at the raised table, Gio's jaw clenched. "Dari ran from me a fortnight past," he said harshly. He refused to let anyone see how broken he felt without her nearness, how anguished he felt by her betrayal, and concentrated instead on his ire. He had thought she had come to have a care for him. Now he realized he had been played for the fool. "I thought her sleeping when in reality she'd fled, so she had a good ten Nuba-hours head start on me."

36

A distant, yet still painful memory flickered through Cam's mind. 'Twas much the same method Kara and Jana had used prior to their ill-fated sojourn away from Tryston. Kara too had feigned sleep, giving her a head start that, sadly, was never recovered. "She's gone off to Galis for a certainty? How can you know this?" he murmured.

Gio's harsh features grew grimmer. "When I followed after her, my path crossed with that of an escaped bound servant—a *male* bound servant from Galis." He shook his head as if he couldn't believe he'd lived long enough to bear witness to such things as male sex slaves. "Leastways, the escaped servant sought me out at Galis' main holo-port and offered me information of Dari in exchange for his safe passage off the matriarchal planet."

"You agreed, I take it."

"Aye. Aye, of course." Gio's jaw clenched impossibly tighter. "The escaped servant swore a vow that he witnessed Dari within the presence of a male humanoid," he gritted out. "A male humanoid named Vrek who stands approximately a *Yeti*-foot shorter than most warriors."

Cam grunted in sympathy. He realized 'twas the last thing in the galaxies Gio would have wished to heard tell of. Dari with another male—possibly being mounted by him— 'twas definitely not the sort of situation a warrior could stomach. If Dari coupled with that male, 'twould drive Gio to death or devolution. Leastways, every time he claimed her body for his use, the scent of the lesser male's would always be there, slowly driving him mad. Once a warrior had a lock on his wench's scent, there could be no other male for her.

Cam waved a hand toward Gio as his thoughts turned in a new direction. "Why did you seek me out afore venturing onward to find Dari?"

"I didn't," Gio admitted. "I immediately set off to track her to the sector the runaway servant claimed to have seen her in." He ran a hand wearily through his black hair and sighed.

"Yet she was gone before I got here. And Galian wenches, tightlipped and secretive as they are, would not tell me in which direction she had headed."

"And their men are too bedamned weak and timid to do aught but their wenches' bidding." Cam's gaze narrowed speculatively. "But I still do not understand why you've come to Zideon, my friend."

"'Twas closer to refuel and rearm myself here than to return to Arak. And," he murmured, "I have not yet told you the whole of it."

Cam felt his stomach muscles clench, though he hadn't any notion as to why. The tiny hairs at the back of his neck stood up, as if portently. "Aye?" he said in low tones. "Tell me then."

Gio sighed. "The male servant espied Dari in the company of someone other than the lesser male's."

"Who?" Cam asked softly.

Gio's gaze clashed with his. "With a golden wench Dari hugged and kissed as though she hadn't laid eyes upon her in nigh unto five Yessat years." His nostrils flared. "With a golden wench she joyfully embraced whilst calling her names such as 'sister' and 'Jana'."

Cam's eyes widened. His hearts rate picked up. If Jana was alive that meant also that —

Nay. Such was not possible.

"What are you saying, my friend." It was a question that had been issued as a statement, for Cam knew exactly what it was that Gio was telling him.

Gio absently raked a hand across his chin. "'Tis possible that your betrothed is alive, Cam. And 'tis possible that my betrothed accompanies her."

38

Chapter Four

Kara was having a wicked-good time watching Dari's jaw hang agape all throughout the evening meal. She knew how her sorely missed cousin felt, for 'twas the same way she'd felt when first she and Jana had arrived on Galis five Yessat years past.

Everything on Galis was different. 'Twas as if the planet was the mirror reflection of Tryston, yet in reverse. In many ways Galis reminded her of a saga her *mani* had once told her about a little girl named Alice and her adventures in a place called Wonderland. Like Alice, they had fallen into a world where everything was the opposite of the world they had once dwelled in.

Dari sighed as she finished the last bit of her stew. She turned to Kara. "Remember the wetted *vesha*-towels the bound servants would hand to us after we partook of a sticky repast?" Her brow furrowed as she studied her sticky hands. "Have they *vesha*-towels here?" she asked almost absently.

Kara grinned. She could scarcely wait to witness Dari's reaction to her answer. "Aye. The male servant attending to you holds yours."

Dari glanced o'er towards him, her lips puckered into a frown much reminiscent of her *mani's*. "I don't see — "

Kara bit down onto her lip to keep from laughing aloud, but the shocked look on Dari's face was nigh unto hilarious. She cleared her throat, grinning from ear to ear. "Do you see it now?"

"Aye," Dari squeaked. She cleared her throat. "I mean aye, I see it." Reaching up, she snatched the wet *vesha*-towel that dangled from the male servant's erect manpart and briskly washed her hands with it. Her nostrils flared. "I don't understand the way of things here, Kara," she grumbled. "And it makes me look the fool."

"Nay." Kara chuckled, a dimple popping out on either cheek. "You look much less the fool than Jana and I did when first we arrived. 'Tis a vow amongst cousins that my jaw hung open for at least a solid fortnight."

Dari found her first grin. A rarity for her, so Kara new she was well-humored. "Aye, I believe it. 'Tis a passing fair place, yet different for a certainty." She glanced back at the male servant attending to her, then turned back to Kara. "How is it possible that..." She waved a hand about. "How do their manparts stay forever erect as they do?"

Kara tossed a *migi*-candy into her mouth, savoring the sweetness of her favored dessert. "They've spells placed o'er their cocks by High Mystiks." She shrugged, having had five Yessat years to grow accompanied to the sight. "'Tis so they are able to perform sexually at any time a wench desires to sample of their charms."

Dari's eyes widened. "Have you ever sampled of their charms?" she murmured.

"Nay." Kara sighed as her teeth sank into another *migi*-candy. "Leastways, I have been tempted a time or two by the sight of so many erect cocks, yet I've never felt as though 'twas the right man or the right time..." Her voice trailed off. "Mostly I've felt it was never the right man," she admitted in a whisper of a breath.

Dari looked away. She didn't wish to think on Gio any more than Kara wished to think on Cam. 'Twas naught but hearts-ache down that *trelli*-paved road.

"I've decided to attend the final hunt of the season," Kara said, turning the topic. "'Tis on the moon-rising of the morrow. Would you like to accompany me?"

"Aye," Dari said, nodding. "I should very much like to—ahh I forgot." She sighed.

Kara's brow furrowed. "What? What is wrong?"

"Kari and I are trekking into Valor City on the morrow. There is...information there I might find useful."

When Dari's features schooled themselves into a grim mask, Kara realized she would say naught else on the subject. She sighed. She wished she knew what it was that her cousin had endured before finding passage to Galis. She wished too that she understood how the six-foot boy-child named Bazi who had accompanied Dari to Galis factored into it. Yet 'twas sorely apparent on both accounts that her cousin cared not to divulge any information as of yet.

But thirty Nuba-minutes later, as Dari rose from the bench to see Bazi off to his rooms, Kara vowed to herself that she would find a way to get her cousin to confide in her. She sensed 'twas important that she did.

* * * * *

Jana's gaze meandered o'er the male servant's body, hovering at the erect manpart holding her *vesha*-towel. 'Twas the biggest, fiercest specimen of manhood she'd ever laid eyes on.

She felt her mouth watering as she gingerly plucked the small towel from his large cock and patted at her lips with it. 'Twould be bliss, the pummeling that cock would give her in her chamber this moon-rising. She'd never taken a male servant to the *vesha* hides, or any other male for that matter, but 'twas for a certainty she would be impaling herself upon the manpart of this formidable male within the hour. She'd never experienced a compulsion so strong, so basic and primal. 'Twas as if her body was being summoned by the goddess to couple with the servant's. "Take yourself off to my rooms," she said arrogantly, not so much as deigning to glance upwards at his face. She feared if she did he would see her bizarre need reflected in her glazed-o'er eyes. "Await me in my bedchamber. I shall be up shortly."

When the male made no move to see to her bidding, she was startled enough to glance up. Leastways, males did not disobey females on Galis—not ever.

Her glowing blue gaze clashed with his piercing silver one. He possessed the eyes of a predator, she thought somewhat warily. The irises of his eyes were the most formidably honed silver she'd ever gazed upon.

And what's worse, the anger radiating from the servant was a tangible thing. She could see the anger in the clenching of his jaw, feel it in the way his eyes bore into hers, sense it as his heavily muscled body corded and tensed. He stood as tall and as big as any warrior, yet she knew from the silver of his eyes that he was no warrior. He was sired of a different species altogether. What species he could have possibly been sired of she hadn't any notion.

Jana forced herself to remember that 'twas her right to avail herself of the servant's charms at any time she so desired. He was but a gift from Klykka and therefore hers for the taking. She narrowed her eyes as she spoke to him. "No matter your species, humanoid, you belong to me for five Yessat years. Klykka captured you fairly in battle and 'tis mine you now are." She kept her words soft, but forceful. "Obey me in all things, handsome one, or 'tis my punishment instead of my pussy that you shall receive."

The servant's jaw clenched hotly. His silver eyes promised retribution. "I beg to differ with you, *mistress*,"—he spat the word out, "but I would not call capturing a drugged and otherwise unawares male in any way fair battling."

Jana waved that away. She didn't know how Klykka had captured him, nor did she care. Her body fair screamed for release just gazing upon him. He elicited primordial reactions from her she'd never heard tell of. The desire to mate with him was so paramount as to be painful. Perspiration dotted her brow as the most intense wave of heat suffused her.

She gasped as her nipples hardened painfully, a reaction that induced one side of the male servant's mouth to curl upwards in an arrogant half-smile. He knew something that she didn't, she thought warily. What in the name of the holy sands was happening to her?

Jana had heard tell of *heeka-beasts* and *gazi-kors* going into heat when the need to reproduce was upon them. Leastways, she had never heard tell of such a thing happening to a Trystonni wench. She was overcome with the need to milk the male's rod with her channel, to allow him to plant a hatchling within her womb...

She gasped at her distressing thoughts, then schooled her features into a formidable mask as her teeth ground together. She would entertain her bizarre thoughts no longer. She needed to mate. 'Twas all that was of importance. "Fair. Unfair. It matters naught for you are mine." Her eyes devoured the length of his swollen cock—a cock Klykka's potent magic had commanded to remain hard at all times— then licked her lips. "Take yourself off to my bed anon, slave." Her eyes found his. "Or I'll have you tied to it."

A tic began to work in his jaw. "If you tie me up, *zya*," he said too softly, "you will know my punishment."

Jana was startled enough to frown. A moment passed in silence, their proverbial horns locking. Then her eyes narrowed determinedly as her jaw did some clenching of its own. "Never threaten your mistress, slave." Her nostrils flared. "Guards!"

* * * * *

Cam strode toward Gio, his stride brisk and efficient.

43

"Well?" Gio asked, his glowing violet eyes scanning Cam's clenched jaw, his flaring nostrils. "Did you learn anything useful?"

"Aye," he bit out. "I did."

Gio sighed. "Kara is alive I take it?"

"Alive and well," Cam growled. "And going by the family name Gy'at Li."

Their gazes clashed as a moment of silence passed between them. Finally, Gio murmured, "Did you get the sector coordinates?"

Cam fisted and unfisted his hand, causing veins to bulge on his forearm. "Aye," he ground out. "I did."

Chapter Five

Kara slithered through the Trefa jungle, naked except for her thigh-high maroon combat boots and the maroon *tishi* paint smeared all o'er her body. She was the only of the Gy'at Li sisters who had decided to partake of the last hunt of the season. The others had made different plans.

Kari, Klykka, and Dari had all three ventured into Valor City in the hopes of gaining an audience with Talia, the Chief High Mystik of Galis. Talia, known amongst the women warriors as Flash for her quick reflexes and unsurpassed skills in pack hunting, held court but twice a Yessat year, this moon-rising being one of them.

Jana had decided to remain behind to bring her wayward and newly acquired male servant to heel, whilst Dorra was still busily enjoying the benefits of teaching Vrek all there was to know in the *vesha* hides.

Thus, the only of the Gy'at Li sisters pack-hunting on this the last official moon-rising of the hunting season was Kara. Leastways, she now wished she hadn't given her vow to do so, for she very much would have preferred trekking into Valor City with her cousin and adoptive sisters o'er gaining more credits to add to their already impressive hoard of them.

Crawling on all fours through the dense jungle's maroon terrain, it occurred to Kara that she had somehow managed to separate herself from the rest of the pack. She sighed, wondering idly when she'd become such a careless huntress. 'Twasn't like her to become distracted for a certainty, yet on this moon-rising she had obviously managed to become distracted enough to wander too far off from the others whilst she tracked the Galian male she'd been hired to bag.

Cam. *He* was the reason, she thought with a harrumph.

Kara had thought back on her former betrothed often o'er the years, hoping against hope that when they met again on the other side of the Rah, he would forgive her of all her transgressions against him. She doubted that he would ever forgive her, even in the next life, yet she had still hoped.

Aye, she had thought back on Cam K'al Ra more times than she could count o'er the years, wondering how he was, hurting herself with jealous thoughts concerning which highborn mistress he might be dallying with, yet during the past fortnight she had been plagued with haunted memories of him stronger than ever before. 'Twas as if her connection to him had been rebirthed. And 'twas driving her mad. She sometimes felt overcome with the need to return to him, knew even that she should, yet she also knew he would always hate her and she didn't think she could bear to see the turquoise eyes that had once glowed with love of the hearts for her glow with naught but revulsion and hatred instead.

Kara took a deep breath and expelled it, deciding 'twas no use in thinking on Cam. What was done was done. She had chosen her own path and she had willingly traveled down it. Like as naught, she would spend the rest of her days regretting that course for she missed her family—and Cam— sorely, yet the past could not be changed. 'Twas all her own doing. She had made choices in her youth and they were choices she must now pay the price for as a wench grown.

The sound of a crackling *tu-tu* frond caused Kara's ears to perk up. She slithered closer to the next brush then came down on her elbows when she neared it, planning to take a look on the other side of it through the gaping hole that always appeared near the bottom of a *tu-tu* bush. Still crawling upon all fours, her naked buttocks were high into the air as she pressed her face closer to the ground that she might glance through the bottom of the *tu-tu* bush and ascertain where the sound had come from.

"Well what have we here," a chillingly cold voice said.

Kara's entire body stilled. She sucked in her breath, knowing precisely who that voice belonged to. She had heard it whisper to her in her every waking fantasy and sleeping dream these past five Yessat years. And right now, it was fiercely angry with her. She felt the anger penetrate her body, sweeping through her in a current of emotion much like a gastrolight charge. The feeling was frightening, and somewhat physically painful. She made a small whimpering noise, then immediately chastised herself for making a sound that could be interpreted as naught but fear and submission.

"Oh aye, you should be afraid," the voice growled as it drew closer.

Kara closed her eyes on a wince, her hearts rate beating rapidly as she quickly tried to think of what she should do. She was frightened—powerfully frightened—and because of that fact she refused to look back at him. Cam K'al Ra had been terrifying to her before she'd disobeyed him. Her fear was a thousand times worse now, knowing he would punish her for a certainty.

In that moment, the past five Yessat years melted away, the rationality of a matured wench along with it. She felt two and twenty again—young and driven by desperation. No matter that she'd missed Cam. No matter that a part of her hearts had secretly hoped this day would come. Now that it was here and she felt the tentative control he had on his emotions threatening to snap, her only thought was to once again flee. Without thinking, her eyes flew open and every muscle in her body corded and tensed as she made a move to lunge to her feet and sprint away.

And yet—nothing happened. Her body remained unmoving. She began to sweat.

"Oh goddess," Kara quietly cried out, feeling somewhat hysterical. Cam's gaze was commanding her body to his bidding. She couldn't move, couldn't flee, could do naught but remain upon the jungle floor on all fours, her face submissively lowered to the ground whilst her buttocks were thrust up high, showcasing her channel for him. Her hearts rate was so high she feared she might do something embarrassingly weak like swoon.

"Now now Kara," the voice said mockingly, "'tis just now that I've found you." Cam drew closer still until Kara was certain he had come down upon his knees behind her. When his large palms settled upon her buttocks, she knew that she had been right. "Don't tell me you think to flee me again so soon," he rumbled out.

Kara's nostrils flared at his superior tone. "If you are so certain of yourself and your abilities, why not release me from your hold that we might decide my fate as equals," she ground out.

When he said nothing for long moments, Kara began to nibble at her lower lip. When she tried to swivel her head that she might look upon him, she found that she couldn't. Even the simple movement of her neck had been summoned, disallowing any part of her body save her voice to move. "Will you not speak?" she asked warily.

Just then she heard a sound, not of Cam's voice, but of his labored breathing. His large hands began to knead her buttocks and she could tell without needing to look upon him that his eyes were feasting on the ripe flesh between her thighs. Perversely, when but a Nuba-second ago she had felt naught but terror at the sheer worrying o'er what he might do to her, she instead felt her nipples harden and her belly clench in anticipation of what he might do next.

"Your channel still drips for me," he murmured as his hands kneaded and massaged the soft globes of her buttocks. He pressed his face against her swollen channel and inhaled the scent of her. "You've been with no male of any species," he rasped out, his happiness apparent in the carnality of his tone. His breathing grew heavier, more labored. "I shall never allow you from my sight again, *pani*." His jaw clenched. "Never."

Kara closed her eyes against what his usage of the word *pani* did to her hearts. How could he respond to her this way? she thought guiltily. How could he call her by the very endearment he'd used for her whilst she'd been growing up on Tryston? After all that she had done to shame him, why would he—

With a groan, Cam buried his face between Kara's thighs and began to lap frenziedly at her channel. "Mmmm," he growled as his tongue streaked wet paths all o'er her flesh. "All mine," he murmured.

Down on all fours and unable to move, with her buttocks submissively raised into the air for him to do to her what he would, she could do naught but shudder and gasp, every fear she'd harbored of him moments past forsaken for pleasure. "Oh aye," she breathed out shakily.

His tongue flicked at her clit in hard, rapid, mind-numbing thrusts and continued to flick at her until she thought she'd go mad. Beads of sweat broke out all o'er her body at the frustration. She wanted him to suck on her, to take her clit into his mouth and suckle hard, yet he continued to toy with her instead, working her up into a delirium whilst knowing she was unable to move to do anything about it.

"*Please*," she gasped, her nipples stabbing out. "Please do not—" She moaned long and loud. "—do not punish me this way."

Cam raised his face from between her legs. His fingers replaced his tongue, rubbing her clit in that maddening way that was firm enough to arouse her, yet too weak to allow for completion. "Make no mistake, *ty'ka*. You will be punished at my hands for a certainty," he said in a low, dark rumble. "Yet no punishments shall be given to you on this the moon-rising of our joining."

Kara's nostrils flared at his arrogant words. She was accustomed to being an independent wench—long accustomed. How dare he inform with such calm stoicism that he meant to punish her *after* they had mated? She would never submit, she thought as her teeth gritted. She would never—

"Oh goddess."

Kara moaned out the platitude when Cam's face dove once more for her flesh, his tongue this time curling around her clit and drawing it into the heat of his mouth. "Suck it," she groaned. "Oh aye—*suck it.*"

With a low growl, he gave her what she wanted, his lips and tongue coiling around the erect little piece of woman-flesh, then frenziedly suckling.

"Aye," she gasped. "Harder."

He suckled her harder, wringing gasps and groans from her. Being unable to move, being unable to do naught but accept the pleasure, made her orgasm come all the sooner. And all the harder.

"*Cam.*"

She came on a loud groan that started low in her throat and worked its way up to her hair and down to her toes. Blood rushed to her face, to her nipples, then he thrust his tongue deeply into her channel whilst she contracted around it.

"*Aye,*" she cried out. "*Oh Cam – aye.*"

Kara closed her eyes and breathed in deeply. The orgasm had been so harsh that she felt shaky and yet the summoning of her body prevented her from shaking. The effect drove her mad. She felt in a frenzy. She needed to move. She needed—something. "Please," she panted out, her entire body tingling almost painfully, "release my body from your summons. I—*ooooh.*"

A bridal necklace was summoned around her neck at the precise moment a long, thick cock slid into her from behind in

50

one fluid motion. She gasped at the sensation of being so full, then moaned when she felt her body being released that she might move about. Immediately, instinctively, she arched up onto her elbows, raised her head, and prepared to look back at him. Unable to refrain from looking upon him any longer, Kara slowly, cautiously, turned her head and raised her eyes to meet his.

She sucked in her breath. She had nigh unto forgotten how powerfully handsome he was. Large and fiercely muscled, golden and perfect, with eyes that glowed a turquoise the likes of which not even vintage *matpow* could compete. Such handsomeness had always been Cam K'al Ra. That visage had caused her to feel lucky as a girl-child, knowing he belonged to her as he did. And yet somehow throughout the years, that feeling of luckiness had been replaced with a fear of him, fear that odd though it was, she no longer felt now that she'd looked upon him as a wench grown.

She had hurt him. 'Twas so apparent in his eyes that the knowledge of it caused yet another stab of guilt to lance through her hearts. Feeling defensive, her nostrils flared as she looked away from him. 'Twas too much pain between them. How could they ever carry on as Sacred Mates?

And then he began to move his cock in and out of her in long, deep strokes, and all her worries were temporarily forgotten on a moan.

"'Tis mine you are, *pani*," Cam said thickly, his voice a rasp. His fingers dug into the flesh of her hips as he rotated his own hips and burrowed into her in a series of slow, mind-numbing strokes. His jaw clenched. "You will never leave me again."

Kara closed her eyes and moaned as she threw her hips back at him. She wanted more. She wanted it faster. Where non-Trystonni females sometimes felt pain upon the loss of their virginity, a Trystonni wench experienced naught but

51

bliss. Why, none could say. "Aye," she breathed out, the sound of their flesh slapping together as much a turn-on as the pummeling itself. *"Harder."* Her breasts jiggled and her nipples stiffened with each hard thrust.

Cam's fingers burrowed deeper into her hips. "Like this?" he asked arrogantly, his thrusts coming harder, deeper, more rapid. "You want this?" he gritted out.

"Oh aye." Kara moaned as she threw her hips relentlessly at him, the need to be pounded into harder and deeper inducing her breath to come out in a hiss. "Fuck me," she ground out in Trystonni. "Fuck me harder."

With a growl he mounted her hard, taking her like an animal as he thrust into her from behind. "My pussy," she heard him rumble out in their tongue. "My pussy."

Kara moaned loudly and wickedly. Their flesh made suctioning sounds as it slapped together. Their breathing was heavy and labored. The sound of him moaning and groaning as he pummeled obliviously into her depths made her belly clench and knot. Being down on all fours made her breasts bounce around wantonly, which sensitized her nipples to the point of pleasure-pain. She knew she was about to come—harder than she'd ever come in her life.

"Caaaam." His name was torn from her lips on a loud moan that echoed throughout the dense Trefa jungle. She threw her hips back at him in a state of near-delirium, greedily wanting fucked as hard and as much as he could give it to her whilst her belly burst and her orgasm tore through her insides. "Oh goddess," she groaned, her hips rocking back and forth. "Aye—oh Cam."

Cam's nostrils flared as he pounded into her mercilessly, holding back nothing. He took her hard, ruthlessly, his teeth gritting as he staved off his orgasm for long minutes, thrusting in and out of the channel he'd been denied for five torturously long Yessat years. "Mine," he ground out o'er and o'er again as he took her. "My pussy."

But then he could endure no more. Kara's moans. Her gasps. The way her flesh sucked him back in every time he withdrew to thrust into her again…

"Kara."

Every muscle in Cam's body corded and tensed as he animalistically pounded into her channel three times more. On a groan that was loud enough to make up for five years outside of twenty Nuba-minutes, he closed his eyes and spurted hot seed deep within her.

It took but three seconds for Kara to understand why a Sacred Mate could pleasure a wench as no other. As her bridal necklace began to pulse, as her belly began to contract with spasms that were nigh unto painful, she threw her head back and moaned whilst they burst together in a maddening peak of euphoria.

Kara felt him gather her into his heavily muscled arms a sheer moment before the blackness came and began to overtake her. She had to wonder at her fate. 'Twas for a certainty that when she woke up she would be long removed from Galis.

As she surrendered to the blackness she could only speculate as to how harsh a punishment she would receive when she woke up.

Chapter Six

Meanwhile, back on Galis...

Jana's nipples hardened as she gazed down upon the chained male servant. The women warriors of her command had laid his eight foot long and heavily muscled body out in spread-eagle fashion, then chained him to the red crystal floor with *boggi*, a set of four shackles that protruded up from the crystal ground. Galians used *boggi* rarely, needing them only on the sparse occasions such as this one when it became necessary to break a recalcitrant male to their bidding.

She took a deep breath as she lowered her gaze to the slave's erect cock. The need to mate with the male, to impregnate her body with his hatchling, tore at her insides until she felt as though she might be crazed. Her breasts heaved up and down as she stood o'er him, her breathing labored.

"Feeling warm, *zya*?" he asked with an infuriating arrogance no slave should feel let alone display.

Jana's nostrils flared. She absently threw a golden tress o'er her shoulder whilst her breasts continued to heave up and down as she stood o'er him. For a certainty she would not answer a question put to her by a slave so bold as this one. And what, she thought idly, did *zya* mean? Twice now he had called her thus.

One night-black eyebrow rose up fractionally as his silver eyes insolently drank in the sight of her naked breasts. "You have delicious nipples," he murmured. "Made for suckling."

Galian wenches always left their breasts unbound, so she was accustomed to her nipples being looked upon, yet the effect this male's possessive gaze had upon her nipples was nigh unto unnerving. They poked out as stiff as she didn't know what, and she wanted them suckled on more than she wanted to breathe. She began to pant—from need and fear. "What manner of species are you?" she whispered. "What magic have you ensorcelled my body with?"

His heavy-lidded eyes were narrowed with lust, with need as powerful as her own. "'Tis no potion or magic trick," he said in a low rumble that brought to mind the growl of a male predator. "'Tis something far more powerful than that, *zya*." His acute silver eyes raked o'er her covered mons, inducing his nostrils to flare. "A *vorah* should never be clothed," he said with irritation. "Remove your *zoka* anon and let me gaze upon you as is my right."

Automatically, Jana's hands rose up to her hips, and her fingers prepared to remove the flimsy, see-through g-string she wore, which on Galis was referred to as a *zoka*. She had to obey him, she thought unblinkingly. 'Twas necessary to obey him in all things. He owned her. He was her master. Her body was his to command. He—

Eh? Yeeck!

Jana shook her head to clear it. She groaned as her hand flew up and clamped to her forehead. She was crazed for a certainty.

Her body, she thought uneasily, felt compelled to obey him. Not merely desirous, but literally compelled. 'Twas as if her brain had been hypnotized and her womb wanted naught but to do the male's bidding.

When she realized that he had been purposely compelling her to think the thoughts he'd desired her to, her lips pinched together in a severe frown as she regarded him from her superior position standing o'er him. "What species are you?" she gritted out. "I would know why it is you are able to mesmerize my mind."

He didn't answer her, and she knew that he wouldn't. At least not yet. "My birth name is Yorin," he murmured, his predator's eyes raking o'er her. "'Tis all you need know for mating me, *vorah*."

Jana's breathing was so labored she thought 'twas possible she might faint. Her need was so great, the desire to mate so powerful, that she felt as though she might die if she didn't impale herself upon his jutting manpart the soonest— this moment.

She tried with every fiber of her being to resist the mental push he was giving her, but in the end his will was too strong to be overpowered. Her hands trembled with the effort of resisting him and a silky sheen of perspiration covered her body as her fingers threaded through the strings of the flimsy blue *zoka* and slowly pushed the g-string down her hips, then lower to her ankles. Her breasts heaving up and down, she stepped out of the *zoka* and stood o'er him naked.

Yorin's sharp silver gaze honed in on her mons, then flicked back and forth between her nipples and the thatch of golden curls between her thighs. "You are mine," he purred, his eyes finding hers, "all mine, *zya*."

Jana closed her eyes briefly, just long enough to drag in a calming breath of air and regain her sanity for a spell. Her eyes flicked open as she warily looked down upon him. "I've changed my mind," she rasped out.

Her breathing grew more and more labored as sexual need turned into acute fear. This male meant to keep her. That he was chained to the floor did naught to quell her anxiety. She needed to remove herself from his presence before she mated him. Somehow, and she knew not how, she was fundamentally aware of the fact that mating him would bind her to him for all times. "I will send the guards to release you," she whispered as she turned on her heel and began to drag herself away. Every step felt heavy, as though crystal weights were tied upon her ankles. "I—oooh."

Jana gasped when a pair of large hands seized her from behind. As he whirled her around to face him, she had little time to digest the knowledge that the chained male had managed to escape his bonds before she found herself being lifted into his arms. 'Twas unfathomable how he had accomplished his escape. Unfathomable and terrifying.

Her eyes widened as she gazed up into his face. Shoulder-length black hair. Piercing silver eyes. A strong jaw.

Silver eyes, she mentally murmured as her gaze narrowed in thought. Silver —

Oh goddess.

"Nay," Jana whispered. She swallowed roughly as her rounded eyes flew wildly up to meet his. "Your species is naught but a legend…" Her voice trailed off disbelievingly.

The look he gave her was arrogant, male. "I am very real, *zya*." Yorin palmed her buttocks whilst he held her and kneaded them as though he had the right of it. "And you are my mate."

Definitive. Unwavering.

Jana's breasts heaved up and down as her breathing grew heavier. "Let me go," she said shakily.

Frightened. Terrified.

Yorin closed his eyes and breathed deeply. His nostrils flared as he inhaled her scent. "Nay," he murmured as his silver eyes slowly opened and clashed with her glowing blue ones. His jaw tightened. "Never."

Jana gasped as an intense wave of heat surged through her, hardening her nipples and inducing her face to flush. She could feel her clit pulsing. Her body screamed for surcease. She knew without a doubt he had done this to her. Or that his nearness had done this to her. She knew naught which. "Release me, Barbarian." It was a plea issued as a command.

He raised her up by the buttocks and slowly, achingly, rubbed her soaking wet labia o'er the hardness of his cock. "Nay," he rumbled out. His callused palms continued to knead her buttocks as he stared down into her face with a dark, brooding intensity. "Impale yourself upon me, *vorah*," he murmured.

Jana moaned as another, stronger, wave of heat suffused her. She knew then and there that he had won. She had to feel him rutting in her — needed his seed implanted in her womb with a compulsion the likes of which terrified her. She could endure no more.

In a series of swift movements, Jana reared up her hips, guided the entrance of her sopping wet flesh to the head of his cock, and bore down hard upon him. She cried out in pleasure as his flesh impaled hers, as his large fingers dug into the padding of her buttocks. Panting, she wrapped her arms around his neck. "Yorin," she breathed out. She felt as though she was in a semi-trance, as though her body was but a vessel doing his bidding. "What do you to me?"

She didn't need to open her eyes to know that his hard silver gaze was drinking in the sight of her parted lips, of her flushed cheeks. She didn't need to see him to be aware of his nostrils inhaling the scent of her as though she smelled of the sweetest Galian perfume.

"I make you mine," he said thickly.

Fill your womb — fill your womb — fill your womb...

The words pounded through her mind, pierced through her hearts, vibrated through every cell of her being, until she felt like an animal — like an all powerful she-beast who would not and could not be stopped.

With a ferocious growl she never would have made whilst mating with any other male, Jana bore down upon his cock once more, and frenziedly began fucking him. Up and down she rode him whilst he held her, moaning and groaning more wantonly than a harem of bound servants.

"Harder," Yorin murmured before nipping at her ear. "Suckle me with your flesh, *zya*."

"Aye," she gasped. Jana's breasts jiggled with every rapid movement, her hips slamming downward in mind numbing strokes.

Seed. She craved his seed. She needed his seed like she needed air to breathe and food to eat.

"*Aye,*" she moaned, the sound of her wet flesh enveloping his. Her hips slammed down harder, faster, more, more, more—

"Harder," he growled, his teeth gritting as her pussy clenched tighter around his cock. "Milk me of seed, Jana."

"*Yorin.*" Jana screamed out his name as she slammed her hips down hard and threw her head back whilst she impaled herself mercilessly. Half groaning and half growling, she was too delirious with the desire to milk his cock to question why it was that she felt a compulsion to bite him. Purely on instinct, her teeth bared and with a she-beast's growl, she bit down hard onto his jugular vein.

"*Zya,*" he groaned loudly, his cock growing impossibly harder within her.

She could feel him tense with pleasure and knowing she had made him feel thusly emboldened her. Jana clamped down as hard as was possible on his jugular vein whilst her flesh made sucking sounds as it enveloped him within her. Slamming down hard upon his erection, her teeth held him tightly whilst she groaned against his neck. Within moments she was bursting, and her channel was frenziedly contracting around him.

"*Zya,*" he rasped, his voice drunk on arousal. He carried her to the raised bed, their bodies never disjoining as he came down on top of her and pounded ruthlessly into her depths.

Jana's teeth held tight to the jugular, pinching the vein together in a way that she somehow knew would drive him to a state as delirious as her own. Yorin moaned and groaned as he pounded into her, his eyes closed in bliss as he mounted her hard.

He rode her long and animalistically, his eyes closed tightly as though he was trying to stave off his orgasm and allow the surrealistic pleasure to go on and on and on. But finally, when he could endure no more, the primordial instinct of his species took o'er, and on a groan loud enough to wake the dead, Yorin burst and he spurted his warm liquid deep inside of her.

Only then, only once her womb had been gushed with potent seed, did Jana release his jugular. Exhausted, and still half delirious, she could only find enough energy to gasp when she felt fangs tear through the flesh of her neck. *"Yorin."*

She came immediately. Loudly. Violently.

Her last conscious thought before the blackness overtook her was that he had bound her to him for life.

And that her womb had been impregnated with a species not her own.

* * * * *

Kari Gy'at Li nibbled on her lower lip as she ended the holo-communication with Klykka. She took a deep breath, breathing in the pure nighttime air of Valor City. Wide-eyed, she turned to Dari. "Kara and Jana are missing."

Dari's eyes rounded to the shape of full moons. *"What?"*

"Kara disappeared from the Trefa jungle a few hours past and Jana seemingly disappeared from her own bedchamber."

"Good goddess," Dari breathed out. Unblinking, she shook her head. "Is there any guess as to what became of them?"

Kari sighed. "Yes." She bit on her lip for a moment as she studied Dari's face. "Klykka thinks they've fled for safety."

"Fled? But why?"

"Because it gets worse," Kari muttered. When Dari looked at her quizzically, she took a deep breath and expelled it loudly. "The Emperor and his men — your father and betrothed included — are demanding that Galis raise its shield and allow them passage inside." Her voice quieted. "They've come looking for Kara and Jana. And," she said pointedly, "you know what else it is that they want as well."

"Me," Dari murmured.

As loathe as she was to admit it, the temptation of surrendering herself to Gio was a bewitching one, yet 'twas for a certainty she could not. Her eyes flicked to a few feet behind them where Bazi stood. 'Twas for a certainty if she was found before she had time to prove who the Evil One was, and what it really was, the young boy-child would be brought back to Arak with her and murdered for a certainty. Mayhap she would be murdered too.

"What do you want to do?" Kari whispered. She reached for Dari's hand and squeezed it in a soothing manner. "Whatever you choose to do, I'll stand by you."

Dari took a deep breath whilst she studied the visage of the six-foot boy-child who for the first time in weeks was at peace. There was but one choice, she knew. Leastways, she could never live with herself if death were to come to him.

Turning back to face Kari, she nodded her head, her mind made up. "We flee. Name the place and let us be gone."

Chapter Seven

Airspace approximately five Nuba-hours outside Planet Zideon,

The next day

Kara sat across from Cam at the raised table aboard the gastrolight cruiser and partook of the evening repast. Or tried to partake of it was mayhap more to the point. She found 'twas hard to enjoy a meal when her only company to share it with stared blankly into space, not so much as deigning to glance in her direction whilst he ate.

She looked away from him and sighed. "Will you not talk to me?" she asked tiredly as she rubbed at a temple with her hand. "'Twill be a long trip if we sit in silence throughout—"

"What is there to say?" he cut in, his voice a low murmur. She could feel his turquoise eyes boring holes into the side of her face, grazing o'er her breasts. "'Tis sorely apparent you've no wish to be my *nee'ka*."

She didn't need to look up and see him to know that his jaw was clenched unforgivingly. "'Tis also sorely apparent to any warrior with half a mind that you will attempt to flee me again when given the chance." His nostrils flared. "And so when we arrive on Zideon you will be granted few, if any, rights. I cannot trust you," he gritted out. "You sentenced me and your birth family to five Yessat years of hellfire with your childishness."

Kara's eyes closed at his words. She felt sick in the pit of her stomach realizing as she did that his words were true. She and Jana had caused much pain for many. 'Twas fact. And yet...

"Why will I be granted no rights?" she asked bitterly, her eyes opening once again then flying up to meet his gaze. She felt a little girl-child again, but refused to show him her weakness. "Think you I have not suffered as w—"

"*Silence.*"

Kara grimaced at the ice in his voice as well as at the strong hurt in his tone. She had shamed him—shamed and embarrassed him. And, she thought with a stab of guilt, she had also betrayed him and hurt him in the doing. Another fiercer stab of guilt lanced through her. "Cam," she said softly, "'tis sorry I am. I never meant to—"

"You never meant to do what?" His jaw clenched impossibly tighter as he slowly rose to his feet. "Hurt me?" he asked softly. He began to walk towards her, the look in his eyes frightening in its intensity.

She would not, she reminded herself, show him her fear. Her nostrils flared instead. "What are you doing?" she asked with more grit than she felt. Her eyes watched him warily. "Mayhap 'tis best do you seat yourself—oh."

Kara swallowed a bit nervously as she studied him through rounded eyes. She gasped when one of his hands clamped about her wrist, then gasped again when he picked her up and carried her o'er to his *vesha* bench. "What do you?" she whispered, her voice slightly shaking.

"I do unto you what is my right. Guards!" he called out loudly. "You may enter this chamber anon."

She sucked in her breath. His voice was like ice and it frightened her for a certainty. When he stretched her out o'er his lap that her head dangled o'er one side of his thighs and her feet o'er the other, her fright escalated into panic. "Nay!" she gasped, unable to believe he was going to punish her this way. "Cam I beseech you—"

"'Tis best," he ground out, "that you accept your token punishment with the grace befitting a Queen." He waited until ten warrior guardsmen had filed into the chamber before he hiked up the back of her *qi'ka* skirt and exposed her bare buttocks to the men of his command. "You knew the price you would pay when you disobeyed me," he gritted. "Verily, I have twice bore witness to the Empress being punished thusly o'er the years. 'Tis the way of it when a wench disobeys her master and well you know it."

Kara closed her eyes, blushing at the impending humiliation. Cam believed her to be aware of her *mani's* public spankings at her sire's hands when in fact she had been kept in the dark. She had heard the rumors. She hadn't believed them — until now.

"Please," Kara said quietly. "I do not wish to be spanked before your men." She bit down onto her lower lip, heat suffusing her face at the mere thought.

"You would have me look the fool after all that you have done?" he asked softly. Too softly, she thought warily.

"Nay but — ouch!"

Kara grimaced at the impact of the first sharp spank he awarded her backside. She steeled herself for the next one, her buttocks clenching together, intuitively figuring as she did that there were four more to come — one for each Yessat year she had spent in hiding.

And, inevitably, she was right. Four more sharp spanks crashed down upon the flesh of her buttocks, each one harder and more painful than the previous one. Throughout the whole of it she managed to retain her quiet dignity in front of Cam and his men, but by the time the last of the five stinging spanks had been awarded to her, her buttocks were fierce sore and she was unable to avoid the release of a small whimper.

His large hand stilled upon the cheek of one red buttock. "Will you disobey me again, wench?" he asked loudly, making certain all in the chamber could hear his words.

Kara felt her teeth grind together at the cool command of his tone. 'Twas no wonder wenches didn't often disobey their Sacred Mates, she thought acidly, for to be splayed out like this and publicly spanked was embarrassing in the extreme. She wanted to curse Cam, to tell him exactly what was on her mind, but she knew that to do so in front of his warriors would only further shame him, which in turn would garner her naught but a fiercer spanking. "Nay," she hissed.

He gave her a small, stinging whack to her backside, letting her know that naught but a properly chastised tone of voice was acceptable. "I did not hear you, *nee'ka*. Answer me again."

Her nostrils flared, but she gave him the bedamned word he sought and spoke it this time in a neutral tone of voice. "Nay," she repeated. 'Twas her guilt and naught else that induced her to say it. And then she added for clarity, "I shan't shame you again."

He ran a soothing hand o'er her buttocks, inducing her to whimper. She gritted her teeth at the submissive sound, chastising herself anon.

"'Tis a good wench," Cam murmured whilst he stroked her buttocks. "Now show these warriors proper respect unto me."

Kara's nostrils flared to wicked proportions. If the rumors concerning public spankings were true, then so too were the rumors concerning how a wench might show proper respect to her Sacred Mate following a punishment. She closed her eyes briefly, realizing as she now did that the spanking was naught in terms of embarrassment compared to what was to come.

For a suspended moment she didn't move, just continued to dangle there across his lap. She flirted with the idea of disobeying him again, but in the end decided against it. Cam needed to save face. And such, whether she had a care for it or not, was apparently how a Trystonni male when shamed by his *nee'ka* restored his pride.

After taking a deep breath, Kara raised herself up off of Cam's lap and stood before him, waiting whilst he summoned off her *qi'ka*. When he had done so, she came down to her knees before him and began to remove the boots that covered his feet.

Cam's eyes raked o'er her body as he watched her perform the ancient ceremony that bespoke of complete and total submission to one's mate. He felt his cock stiffen merely watching her and wanted more than anything to fill her up with it.

In front of him, Kara's cheeks were pinkened. Mayhap, she told herself, if her mating mistress had informed her of this custom years ago whilst she had been of the schooling age, she never would have been so bold as to flee Tryston in the first.

"Show them," Cam murmured. "Show these warriors your submission to me."

Her eyes widened at the challenge she heard in his voice. This was his way of saying that if she was truly sorrowful o'er the pain and shame she had caused him in the past, then she would cause no more by shaming him yet again in front of his men.

On a sigh, she relented.

Naked on her knees before him, Kara spread out her thighs as far apart as they would go, then lowered her face to his bared feet. She was careful to keep her channel on full display for the warriors gathered behind her to watch, her buttocks raised high as she began kissing his feet.

She knew 'twas up to Cam how long this phase of her punishment was to go on and, indeed, he allowed it to go on for quite some time. Perversely, 'twas only then that Kara realized just how sorely she had injured him. Cam was not the type to inflict revenge upon her, yet the fact that he was allowing the kissing of his feet whilst her channel was on display for others to go on for so long was proof positive of all that he had endured at her hands. She grimaced at the thought, wondering if even after all this had transpired he would forgive her.

"Enough," Cam murmured. "Rise up, *nee'ka*."

She closed her eyes at the gentleness of his tone. 'Twas then that she knew for a certainty that he had harbored no desire to see her splayed out the way that she had been. He had merely done it because 'twas what was expected of him. To do aught else would have made him appear weak—a death sentence for a warlord who forged his way in life by commanding the respect of so many.

Mayhap 'twas guilt, mayhap 'twas the desire to show him she well and truly wished for peace between them, but when Kara raised herself up before him, she lifted only her face and remained upon her knees. Her thighs still spread submissively wide, her channel still on display for all and sundry to gaze upon, she removed his thick cock from his leathers and wrapped her lips about it.

Cam shuddered, his breath escaping in a hiss. He cupped her face with his palms, watching through eyes narrowed in bliss as she sucked him off for all to see. She took her time with it, allowing him to feel the pleasure of her warm mouth for long minutes before she began working him frenziedly, suckling his stiff erection in rapid sucks.

He came hard, spurting into her mouth on a groan. His breathing labored, he flicked his hand toward his men, indicating 'twas time for them to take their leave.

At last, Kara's head slowly raised from his lap and their gazes clashed together. Cam's nostrils flared as he studied her face, wanting as he did for all to be healed between them, yet simultaneously afraid to entrust her with his vulnerability.

Kara took a deep breath as she studied his face in return. Everything Cam had punished her for—and more—was true. She had hurt and betrayed both him and her family. She had fled from her husband without giving him the chance to calm her fears of him. She had schemed and lied, connived and even stolen to achieve her means. There was much she had done that was wrong. And yet, there was one thing her Sacred Mate was wrong about himself.

"I won't try to run from you again," she said gently. "I say that now not that you might save face before your warriors, but that you might know in your hearts 'tis true." Her eyes softened as she looked at him. "'Tis a vow amongst Sacred Mates."

He looked away from her, afraid to believe. "As if a vow from you means aught," he defensively ground out.

Affronted, Kara sucked in her breath. She quickly stood up and backed away from the raised table a few steps. "There is much I have done that is wrong," she rasped out, her naked breasts heaving before him, "leastways, I have never uttered a lie unto you."

The hurt in her voice caused Cam to look up. He studied her face but said nothing.

"Even once in the five years you thought me dead," she asked angrily, "did you ever wonder why 'twas that I ran from you?" She didn't wait for an answer. "I wanted a taste of freedom, aye, but I've come to realize o'er the passing of time that freedom wouldn't have been enough of a lure to make me flee."

His nostrils flared. "Oh aye, *nee'ka*, I know why 'twas you fled from me. Leastways, it's all I've been able to think upon every moon-rising for the last five Yessat years."

Kara squinted her eyes and cocked her head. She could tell he was serious in his thinking, yet something told her they were not thinking along the same lines. His voice was too bitter. "What mean you?" she whispered.

"Because I was not a warrior born," he ground out. Cam's eyes bore into hers. "I spent year upon year upon year proving myself to be a better hunter, a better fighter, than any highborn warrior in existence." His eyes flicked longingly o'er her form. "I did so that you might be proud to call me your own, that you would feel pride of the hearts instead of embarrassment for being Kara K'ala Ra." He looked away. "Yet all that I did 'twas never enough. You never felt pride. And you never came to love me," he murmured.

A numbing chill worked its way down Kara's spine. She couldn't have been more shocked by his confession had he sprouted metallic skin and turned into a *gazi-kor* right there at the raised table. Her eyes haunted, she took a deep breath. "'Tis ironic for a certainty," she whispered as she stared at him.

"I don't follow." Cam shook his head, then looked up to meet her gaze once more. "Of what do you speak?"

"'Tis my sire that wanted you to be a great warlord, but 'twas never what I myself wanted."

His brow furrowed uncomprehendingly.

"I ran from you because I feared I was naught but a battle prize to you," she said sadly. "It had naught to do with your titles or lack thereof."

Cam's entire body stilled. Every muscle in his body corded and tensed. He wanted so much to believe her for he loved her as he could love no other, and yet so much hurt had passed between them that he was afraid to cling to the small hope she'd just thrown his way. "Do you speak the truth to me?" he rasped out.

Her smile was poignant, sad. "Aye, 'tis true."

She took a deep breath, too overcome with emotion to remain in the chamber with him. She needed to go to her apartments aboard the ship and think for a spell.

She loved Cam K'al Ra. She had always loved him. She had tried to forget it for a time, yet she could suppress the truth of it no more. And now, ironic though 'twas when at last she had admitted her buried feelings to herself, it appeared as though all was lost. He didn't trust her. He didn't believe her. And mayhap he never would again.

Kara turned about to walk away. She could feel his eyes upon her. Swiveling her head, she took a calming breath and then looked at him from o'er her shoulder. "You became a great warlord that I might love you," she said quietly. "Yet 'twas the son of a lowly *trelli* miner that I fell in love with."

Cam felt tears sting the backs of his eyes. He blinked them away as he watched her take a deep breath and walk away from him. It hadn't escaped his notice that her eyes had been glowing a dimmed blue, believing as she did that all was lost between them.

Leastways, she was wrong. Things had never felt more right.

Or at least, he conceded wearily, they had never felt more right to him. How she felt about him now, he couldn't say.

Chapter Eight

Meanwhile, back on Galis…

Zor's lips tightened into a grim line as he glanced around at the bevy of bound male servants attending to the evening repast. 'Twas nigh unto disgusting, the sight of so many erect manparts standing about. He sighed, telling himself 'twas true he had now lived to see it all. And to think that his wee Kara had lived amongst the Galians for five Yessat years…

As his beloved *nee'ka* would say, good grief.

Zor rubbed his weary temples as he listened to his brother Dak put questions to the High Mystik of the Gy'at Li sector. 'Twas going to be a long moon-rising, he decided on a martyr's sigh. He was anxious to leave, anxious to take his *nee'ka* to Zideon that they might be reunited with their hatchling. Yet he was also of a mind to know that wee Jana and Dari were passing fair.

"I want," Dak ground out, "to have my hatchlings back anon." His nostrils flared. "I do not believe for even a Nuba-second that you've no idea where they've gone off to."

Klykka's eyebrows rose at his imperious tone, but she said nothing of it. "Mayhap if you warriors had shown a care for their feelings whilst growing up they never would have fled to begin with."

"I was given no choice," Dak gritted, pausing in his speech long enough to throw a sour look Zor's way. "I had to remove Dari to Arak. Leastways, this talk is all for naught. Your Emperor has issued you a direct order and 'tis for a certainty you *will* obey it."

"You are lucky, wench," Kil hissed, his eyes narrowing at the High Mystik from where he was seated next to Lord Death across the raised table, "that my brother did not sentence you to the gulch pits for your treason." He flung an arm about wildly. "You aided and abetted the escape of three royal hatchlings!" he shouted. "Our family has grieved Kara and Jana's 'passing' for o'er five years." He slashed his hand through the air. "For a certainty you would be gulch beast food if I were Emperor."

Klykka rolled her eyes, not at all intimated. "I shall praise the holy sands that you are not then," she said dryly.

Kil merely grunted.

Klykka schooled her features into a fashionably bored mask. In truth, she was more than a wee bit frightened. Not for her own fate, for she knew she had been within the rights of the Holy Law to aid wenches she believed to be political prisoners on their home planet, but more so she was worried for Dari, Jana, and Kari. She hadn't been telling untruths when she'd declared to the warriors that she had no clue as to their whereabouts. A gastrolight storm the moon-rising prior had sizzled out the main holo-communicator within her stronghold and the last she'd heard from the women warriors of her command, 'twas still not functioning properly. And so, 'twas truth she had no notion as to their position.

Leastways, the High Mystik told herself, she could do naught but try to distract the warlords, and hope against hope that her stalling would provide enough time for the lot of them to flee Galis. She prayed to the goddess that they had not yet been caught, sending up a quick plea to Aparna to humbly ask for her omnipotent intervention. These warriors, she thought acidly, considered naught but how the absence of the wenches affected *them*. If she was forced to endure one more diatribe on the rights of a Sacred Mate or the rights of a sire, she would like as naught gag.

Klykka sat up straighter on her *vesha* bench, her dark eyes narrowing seductively as she ran a tongue across her lips. When the nipples of her unbound breasts began to harden and elongate of seemingly their own volition, Zor narrowed his eyes.

"Stop it," he grunted.

She batted her eyelashes as if innocent. "Stop what, Excellent One? I am but your humble servant thinking to entertain you in the proper, traditional Galian manner."

He harrumphed at that. "You think to distract us more like."

Klykka pretended to be shocked. "Whatever do you mean?" she asked in a tone of voice sweeter than *migi-candy*.

Kil grunted, his eyes narrowing. "Thrice you have been issued a direct command to tell us where the Q'ana Tal hatchlings are hidden, and thrice now you have answered us by bringing us to peak." His jaw clenched hotly. "I do not wish to be brought to peak!" he bellowed.

When it occurred to him what he had just said, he felt his cheeks redden. When the warriors gathered about began to uncomfortably clear their throats, said cheeks flamed from red to scarlet. "Leastways," he sniffed, "my leathers are fair soaked from the last two times. 'Tis hard to find replacements for them so far removed from Morak," he finished dumbly.

Zor rolled his eyes.

Klykka paid neither warrior any heed whatsoever. She threw a long black tress o'er her shoulder, then stood up and removed the bottom to her *zoka*. The warriors moaned when they felt her telekinetically send out sexual pulses, then groaned when she began to massage her nipples as she slowly walked towards Jek Q'an Ri, Kil's commander.

"Oh nay," Dak said hoarsely as he closed his eyes tightly, "the wench thinks to impale herself upon our cousin's rod this time."

Zor whimpered. "'Twas a hard enough spurt the last time. And that with naught but a mental push."

Kil's head fell back on a groan. "'Tis for a certainty we shall sleep for hours rather than minutes this time." He clamped a hand to his forehead. "I pray to the goddess that Mari packed me a fresh pair of leathers."

"Geris will know," Dak said grimly. "Leastways, she knows everything." He moaned as another wave of sexual titillation was sent his way. "'Twill be the war of wars when I remove myself to Ti Q'won."

Zor's eyes began to roll back in his head. "If the erotic arts performers who ventured into Sand City had been so talented, I would have expired before ever I'd set out to capture my *nee'ka*." He moaned grimly. "Where is Kyra when I need the wench? She and Rem have been removed to Valor City o'er long."

Their chatter turned into fierce groans as they watched the naked High Mystik run her fingers through Jek's mane of hair. Their cousin tried to remain strong, tried to fight off the desire to couple with Klykka, but being unmated…'twas looking as though 'twas mission impossible.

Jek's gaze ran o'er the length of the High Mystik. "Stop it, wench," he hissed. "You will tell the Emperor anon where the hatchlings are."

Klykka ignored him, deciding instead to remove his cock from his leathers. "Oh," she breathed out. "'Tis exceedingly large." She licked her lips, meaning the compliment. No males within her harem were possessed of such huge manparts.

Jek gritted his teeth when she cupped his balls and began massaging them. His cousins had long teased him that he was the wiliest warrior amongst them for 'twas common to find his rod buried within a hot channel at any given time. Whenever none within the Palace of Mirrors could find him, they knew to check within the harem chamber. If he was not training or warring, 'twas where he could always be found. Yet now his strong need was working against him. He needed to resist her. If only he could distract—

Jek sucked in his breath when the wench wrapped her lips around the head of his cock. Her hands continued to massage his man sac whilst her tongue suctioned his shaft into the heat of her mouth, taking him all the way in until he could feel the back of her throat. His nostrils flared. "Cease this," he hoarsely commanded her.

"Mmm nay." Klykka closed her eyes and enjoyed the feel of him, speaking on the subject no more. She loved cocks. She loved sucking them and fucking them. 'Twas why she was forever battling, finding more to add to her collection of bound servants. But warriors...Galian wenches went out of their way to avoid them, so 'twas a rare treat indeed to suckle a cock so large and thick. She intended to savor the moment.

Jek groaned as he watched his shaft disappear into the High Mystik's mouth, o'er and o'er, again and again. Down on her knees before him, her head bobbing up and down upon his lap, he couldn't resist the urge to watch her work upon him. And so before he could think better on it, his hand moved to grasp her dark hair, and he brushed it out of her face that he might watch her suckle of him. "Good goddess," he breathed out.

She was like an animal. Klykka sucked harder and harder, faster and faster, her eyes closed in bliss, her throat issuing primitive moans whilst she feverishly worked up and down the length of him. The sucking sounds her lips made coupled with her extreme talent at doing so, made his jaw clench tightly. As if on instinct, his hands reached down for her breasts, and he cupped them whilst he massaged her nipples and watched her mouth devour him.

"Oh aye." Klykka's head bobbed up into his line of vision when the nipple massage became too arousing to continue suckling him. Naked, she climbed up onto his lap, gasping at the sensual jolts going through her. "Tug at them," she whispered, arching her back that her chest was thrust closer to him. "Please."

Beads of sweat broke out upon Jek's forehead. He wanted to stop, wanted to keep her from causing the room to pass out in a fit of peak, yet the arousal she was experiencing was being transferred to him, making him feel the same way, making him crave more and more, making him want—nay need—to bury his cock deep inside of her body. He could hear the moans of the warriors around him and knew that he had to remain strong.

The High Mystik smiled slowly, knowing as she did that his trying was all for naught. "'Tis no use, handsome one," she whispered as she cupped one of her breasts and ran her elongated nipple o'er his lips. "Open up for me. 'Tis impossible to resist and well you know it."

Jek's nostrils flared at the taunt. He removed his lips from her nipple. "Cease your witchery," he said thickly.

The nipple looked so ripe, so suckable, so hard and delicious. He gritted his teeth. "Cease this anon." Each word became quieter, less forceful.

She grinned. "I have studied the art of peaking for more Yessat years than you've been alive, feisty one." Her dark eyes narrowed, glazing o'er in passion as they found his glowing blue ones. "Suckle me," she murmured as she ran the tip of her nipple o'er his lips again. "You are not mated. I can give you pleasure as no other ever has," she breathed out.

Jek felt as though he was going mad. He was a warrior. Nature had declared that his sexual need would always be great. He was torn between instinct and duty. 'Twas torture, this.

His breathing grew labored as he felt his large hands clutch her fleshy buttocks and dig into them. Before he could stop himself, his mouth opened and his tongue darted out to curl around the High Mystik's nipple.

"Mmm aye," she said on a breathy moan. She began to rock her hips atop his lap, the entrance of her wet channel running o'er the head of his engorged manhood.

Jek's nostrils flared, his jaw clenched, and yet he could no sooner stop breathing than stop sucking on her nipple. He drew the piece of elongated flesh between his lips and firmly sucked it from root to tip, o'er and o'er again. Her moans made his stomach muscles clench. Her soaking wet cunt continued to tease the head of his manhood, until he felt as though he'd die on the spot if she didn't impale herself upon him.

The torture of fighting her combined with the torture of wanting her was making him delirious. Teasing him—she kept teasing him. The engorged flesh of her channel kept stroking o'er his cock, promising to envelop him within but never doing so. He had to fight her, he thought desperately. He had to—

"Just do it," he heard Kil groan from across the chamber. "Take her and get it o'er with."

'Twas all the justification he needed. Tearing his mouth away from her nipple, he growled low in his throat, surprising a gasp out of the High Mystik. She sucked in her breath as he clutched her hips, then groaned long and loud whilst he sheathed himself fully within her flesh.

"Aye," Klykka moaned, her eyes closing as he used his large hands to force her hips down upon him in deep, rapid strokes. Her breasts jiggled with each thrust, sensitizing them all the more. Against his large frame she knew she looked like naught but a doll, riding up and down the length of his huge shaft. The thought turned her on all the more, so she threw back her head and bounced away upon him, gluttonously loving every moment of the impaling. "Harder," she panted. "More."

Jek gave up the fight entirely, the nature of his species taking o'er to revel in the feel of her tight, milking flesh wrapped about him, preparing to contract about him. "Aye," he murmured, his teeth gritting. "Reach your pleasure upon me."

Klykka gasped as she rode him, her moans coming harder and louder as she bounced up and down. Her clit was stimulated with each down stroke, which in turn hardened her nipples further and induced need to knot in her belly. She could hear their flesh slapping together, could smell the heady scent of their combined arousal. When his tongue curled once more around her nipple and drew it back into his mouth for a suckling, she could take no more.

"Aye," she cried out, her hips rocking deliriously against him. Another fiercer contraction tore through her, and she screamed as her entire body clenched and then convulsed atop him.

Jek gritted his teeth, the sexual flickers her peaking sent out catapulting him into a near maddened state. He groaned low in his throat as his fingers dug into the flesh of her hips, then spurted his warm liquid within her on a growl.

All throughout the chamber, warriors convulsed and moaned. On Klykka's third, final, and harshest peak, moans turned into tortured groans as the entire room orgasmed, then passed out.

Breathing roughly, Klykka smiled down at Jek. Unable to resist touching him before climbing off his big body, she bent her head and sipped softly at his lips. Telling herself there was no time to lose, she removed his manhood from her pussy with a suctioning sound, then scrambled to her feet.

Her eyes darted toward the crystal staircase above. She glanced back at the chamber of passed out warriors once more to make certain all were in deep slumber before she darted toward the twisting stairs, taking them two at a time as she ran up.

She had to find her sisters via the holo-communicator. She could only pray the wenches of her command had fixed it whilst she'd been busily stalling.

* * * * *

Kyra's lips pinched together in a frown as she gazed down at her snoring husband. Her eyes narrowed in confusion when she took note of the large wet stain permeating the pair of leathers he wore. Crouching down to touch them, her nostrils flared when she realized it was semen.

"What the hell is going on?" she bit out to Rem without looking up at him. "Why are all of these warriors passed out?" She huffed as she glanced around. "And why are all of them wet from their own orgasms?"

Rem sighed. "It looks as though the High Mystik sought to stall their questions."

Kyra harrumphed, her arms crossing under her breasts. "It looks like she did better than stall them. It looks as though they've been knocked completely out of commission for a while now."

"Aye."

She harrumphed again, then began gently slapping at Zor's face in the hopes of rousing him. "Wake up," she chided him. "Please Zor—wake up!"

When five Nuba-minutes had passed by and her husband continued snoring as loudly as ever, she gave up with a groan. "Now what do we do?" She looked up at Rem. "Where is the High Mystik anyway?"

Rem's gaze was narrowed thoughtfully. "I know not for a certainty," he murmured. "But I think I've a lock on her. We had best go find her."

Kyra studied his face for a suspended moment. She knew he still hadn't totally recovered from his brush with devolution. Almost, but not quite. The result being, she reminded herself, that he sensed things a lot clearer than the average warrior did. Like an animal, his hearing was keener, his sense of smell more acute. If he thought he'd located her, then he probably had.

"Okay," she said as she made to stand up. "I'm right behind — oomph."

Kyra sighed as she lost her balance and landed flat on her rump. "These damn boobs," she muttered as she came up onto her knees and held a hand out to Rem for aid. "How many more years of not bearing children do I have left until they go away already?"

Rem chuckled. "Mayhap just a few more, sister." He took her hand and pulled her up to her feet. "Gis is the exact opposite of you. She nigh unto worships her moosoos."

Kyra shook her head and grinned. "How many children do the two of you have now? Twenty? Thirty?"

"Eight," Rem said proudly. He guided her toward the staircase. "All sons save Zari."

Kyra looked up the long, twisting flight of stairs and sighed dejectedly.

Rem wiggled his eyebrows. "Too much effort with the moosoos?"

"Yes," she said forlornly.

He was preparing to sweep her up into his arms and carry her, when the sound of the warriors coming-to caught up with them. They both turned around and watched them.

Kyra's lips puckered into a tight-lipped frown as she studied Zor. His hair was a mess, his big body stretching and yawning, as he roused himself from what looked like a ten-year slumber. When at last their gazes clashed, she saw his cheeks go up in flames.

"'Tis about time you arrived, *nee'ka*," Zor said defensively as he took to his feet. "Leastways," he sniffed, "'twas wicked-bad torture that the High Mystik put us all through."

Kyra rolled her eyes. "Gimme a break."

Zor blushed profusely but said nothing. "Stay down below whilst we search for the nefarious Klykka," he mumbled. His gaze shot back to the raised table where the male servants were starting to regain consciousness. "And stay away from those bedamned males whilst I'm searching," he grumbled.

* * * * *

"Hurry!" Klykka ordered the woman warrior who was fiddling with the holo-communicator. "We've no time left. Those bedamned warlords will wake up the soonest and they will like as naught be feeling surly." Her nostrils flared as she paced back and forth within the war-planning chamber. "This is taking far too long!"

"'Tis sorry I am, Your Worthiness," the warrior woman demurred. "I am working as fast as I—ahh here we go."

Klykka took a deep breath and released it. "Send out a distress call to Kari's communicator anon."

The High Mystik resumed her pacing whilst she awaited a signal to come back from Kari. She knew 'twas a race to the finish line for if those warlords woke up before she spoke to her sister she would never get another chance to warn her. Finally, after a gut-wrenching two Nuba-minutes had ticked slowly by, the holo-screen on the far wall lit up and Kari and Dari's faces shown through.

"Thank the goddess," Klykka breathed out. "Are the deuce of you passing fair?"

Kari tucked a tress of fire-berry hair behind her ear. "Yes. I was worried when I couldn't get through. Is everything alright there? Was Jana found? And are you and Dorra—?"

Klykka interrupted her questions with a wave of her hands. "We've no time for this. In a few words," she said hurriedly, "Dorra and I are passing fair, yet Jana has not yet been located. Kara was captured by her betrothed—" She ignored their gasps and continued on, knowing time was of the essence. "And I've a great hall full of passed out warlords, all of whom want to find Jana and Dari." She tugged in a breath of air. "Are the deuce of you safely removed from Galis with the boy-child?"

"Aye." Dari nodded succinctly, answering the question for Kari. "Bazi sleeps the sleep of the innocent whilst Kari steadily navigates us from Trek Mi Q'an."

"Where do you go?" she asked quickly. "Tell me that I might send aide."

Just then the doors to the warring chamber exploded open and angry warlords materialized seemingly out of nowhere. Klykka whirled around and gasped, startled. Thinking quickly, she closed her eyes, preparing to send out the strongest wave of sexual titillation in existence. "Nay!" she bellowed when Jek's strong hands clasped her arms and forced her to cease her mental incantations. "Release me!"

"'Tis best if you remain silent, wench," Jek murmured into her ear. "You've already made me look the fool. I shan't hesitate to return the favor."

Klykka gulped a bit nervously, but said nothing.

Her body in fight-or-flight mode, Kari was preparing to end the holo-communication so their position couldn't be traced when a sight she had not at all been expecting to see appeared before her. Her eyes wide, her face draining of all color, she gasped as her silver-blue gaze raked over a very familiar and very imposing eight-foot tall frame. "You," she breathed out as her eyes found his face.

Death's entire body stilled as his golden gaze drank in the sight of Kari Gy'at Li for the first time in nine agonizingly long Yessat years. He felt as though he'd been punched in the stomach so powerful was the effect on him. He had scoured Galis and searched the dimensions for her these past years, yet until this moment had never heard tell of her. "You disobeyed me, wench," he rumbled out, his jaw clenched tightly. He ignored the feelings she evoked in him and concentrated on the tangible. "Come back here anon and bring the princess with you."

Kari said nothing. She was so stunned that she could scarcely think let alone speak. Her eyes narrowed as they raked over him. He looked so powerful, so masculine and handsome. His huge, massively muscular body looked to be riddled with even more battle scars than he'd sported since the last time she'd seen him.

She sighed. She'd fantasized about him for nine Yessat years. And now here he was.

Taking another deep breath, Kari closed her eyes briefly and snapped herself back into the proper frame of mind. She wanted to see him, wanted to touch him so incredibly much, but…

"I can't," she whispered, looking away from him. "I can't come back."

Death's eyes narrowed at her words. "Do not flee from me again, little one, or when I catch you 'twill be hellfire to pay," he finished grimly.

Her eyes flew open. "Why?" she asked hoarsely. "Why do you want me? For a toy to add to your collection?"

Death's golden gaze never wavered from Kari's. "You are mine," he said firmly to Kari. "You are my mate."

Klykka gasped. Stunned, and uncertain what to say, she joined in the conversation for the first time. "This matters naught, Kari, and well you know it." Her nostrils flared. "Dari has a mission at hand and naught, not even emotions, can interfere with it," she reminded her.

Kari nodded, but didn't open her eyes.

Kil's gaze widened as it flew to Dari. "What does she mean, Dari? What has happened? Of what mission does she speak?"

Dari nibbled at her lower lip and looked away.

"You can tell me, Dari," Rem chimed in. "You and I were ever close whilst you were growing up. Come, *pani*, tell us—"

His words were interrupted by the crashing sound of Dak making his way into the Gy'at Li warring chamber. Dari cried out when she saw him, her usual formidable resolve crackling under the emotion of seeing her sire once again.

Dak came to a halt in front of his daughter's holo-image and took a deep breath. His eyes raked o'er her, ascertaining that she was passing fair. "*Mani* and I are worried," he rasped out. His eyes were troubled. "Please remove yourself to Arak, *ty'ka*."

"I can't," Dari said quietly, her glowing blue eyes in mourning. "I can't chance it until I have...more information." She swore under her breath, immediately chastising herself for giving away even that much of a hint to her sire as to her activities. She could take no chances.

Dak's brow furrowed in confusion. "Information?" he murmured. "What sort of information do you seek, *pani*?" When she did naught but remain rigid in her silence, chills raced up and down Dak's spine. He knew—knew—something horrid had happened and mayhap was still happening. "Please, wee one," he said pleadingly, "I can't help you if you don't—"

Her sire's words were brought to a halt a moment later when Gio stormed into the warring chamber and made a direct path toward Dari's holo-image. To her credit she held his gaze, even though he looked as though he wanted to murder her. He was angry, she realized. Fiercely possessive and angry.

"Remove yourself back to Arak," Gio ground out. His eyes grazed o'er her, the longing he felt to simply touch her overwhelming to him. His nostrils flared. "Do not make me hunt you down, *ty'ka*."

Dari's nostrils did some flaring of their own. She ignored the sunken feeling she had inside, ignored her reaction to the way her hearts thumped in her chest when he called her *ty'ka*, ignored the chance she'd been given to gaze upon him once more, ignored even the memories that pounded through her mind, reminding her of the wondrous way he'd been intimately touching her body ever since her seventeenth Yessat year had passed. She reminded herself instead of how she'd loathed him when first she'd been taken to Arak so many Yessat years ago. 'Twas necessary to call upon those emotions now. "You shan't find me until I am ready to be found, Gio Z'an Tar." She took a deep breath. "If ever I want found."

A tic began to work in his cheek. "You would cause this much grief to experience naught more than a time of freedom? Have you not learned by Kara's example?" he murmured.

Dari sat up regally straight, her chin going up a notch. He *would* attempt to remind her that even though Kara had fled, in the end she had been recaptured by Cam.

Well, 'twas no matter, she reminded herself firmly. Her sire and uncles had nigh unto choked a confession out of her, but now that she'd regained her wits, 'twas necessary to remember she had to keep Gio in the dark. Let him think she desired naught but freedom. Let him think what he would if it kept him from the Rah.

Just then Bazi awoke and the masculine sound of his voice calling to Dari captured the attention of every warlord in the chamber. Dari gulped a bit roughly, uncertain what to do. She wanted no one, not even her sire, let alone an entire chamber of warriors, to know that Bazi was aboard ship.

Gio's entire body stilled, for he knew not whom the voice belonged to, only that it was male. His breathing grew labored as he narrowed his gaze at his betrothed. "Who is that?" he rasped out. "And why does the male beckon to you?"

Dari took a deep breath, but remained silent.

"Answer me wench!" Gio bellowed, his arm flailing wildly about. A low growling sound erupted from his throat a split second before he hurled himself toward the holo-image as if trying to jump through it. "I'll kill him!" he shouted. "Do you hear me, Dari? You have issued your lover a death sentence!"

Dari's eyes widened and then closed. Good goddess, what should she do? What should she—

Dak and Kil surged toward Gio in an effort to restrain him. Dari's hand flew to grasp Kari's wrist and her fingers dug into the flesh there whilst she watched the fight unfold. Gio had gone wild. Primal. She knew how strong her uncle and sire were, yet 'twas not until Lord Death and her Uncle Rem added their strength into the mayhem that Gio was successfully restrained.

Dari released a pent-up breath, then released Kari's wrist a moment later. She knew 'twas impossible for Gio to jump through a virtual image, yet she didn't want him to do himself a harm trying either.

"Cease this," Dari said fervently. "Please, Gio, do not do this," she said in a tone of voice that coming from any other wench would have sounded a plea.

His breathing was heavy, his chest constricting up and down with the movement. Restrained by two warlords at either side, he could do naught but stare into her eyes. "How could you hurt me this way?" he rasped out. His eyes were wild, panicked, as though he had to recapture her anon lest he go mad. "I thought you had…come to love me." His voice was hurt. Choked and hurt.

Dari closed her eyes briefly and took a deep breath. She wanted to scream at the fates that had made it necessary to tear out his hearts this way. She yearned to shout out to him that 'twas not true, that she had coupled with no male, yet an inner voice kept telling her to remain silent until Bazi was safely removed from Trek Mi Q'an.

Gio's jaw clenched. "Have you naught to say?" he ground out.

Dari held his gaze for a suspended moment. 'Twas so quiet within the warring chamber that nary a breath was taken. But finally, realizing 'twas naught that could be said whilst she needed to protect Bazi, she gently shook her head and looked away.

"I see," he murmured.

For the first time in she didn't know how long, Dari felt her eyes filling up with tears and her bottom lip trembling. Before she could disgrace herself, before she began weeping right there in front of all and sundry, she stood up and left the chamber she had been seated within, leaving Kari to deal with the situation alone.

Dari could hear Gio yelling for her as she walked away. She could feel his panic, wondering as he must where she was walking off to…or *whom* she was walking off to. She could feel his anger, his hurt, his possessiveness, his sense of betrayal. Weeping, she fled as fast as her feet would carry her.

Back at the holo-communicator, Kari sighed. This was the most confusing and gut-wrenching day she'd lived through ever since that day so many years ago when forces she still didn't comprehend had snatched her from earth and placed her on Galis. Her mind said that they were doing the right thing, yet her body and heart wanted to return to Galis...and to *him*. It was obvious that Dari was experiencing the same emotions. She took comfort in that, realizing she was not alone.

Kari gazed into Death's golden eyes once more. The intense way that he stared at her told her he would never let this decision go unchallenged. He would hunt her down, she realized. He would never stop, never relent, until he had her firmly under his power once more.

Heat rushed through her as the renewed memories of the week they had spent together in Crystal City took over. The way he had touched her, commanded her, and perhaps...loved her?

She sighed, knowing that week could never again be relived.

Closing her eyes and taking a fortifying breath, she switched off the holo-communicator.

Chapter Nine

Planet Zideon, Kopa'Ty Palace

A sennight later

Cam lie abed, moaning as he watched his cock disappear into the mouth of his ever-voracious *Kefa* Muta. He wanted Kara, would give anything to have her lips wrapped about his manhood thusly, yet knew also that he would have to content himself with his favored slave. Kara had made that plain when she'd sent Muta to his rooms to see to his comforts this eve. For a sennight now she had done the same every moon-rising, not deigning to see to his needs herself.

He gasped as he spurted, his eyes closing tightly as he pretended 'twas the mouth of his *nee'ka* he was spurting into. He needed to see her, needed to touch her, yet was afraid 'twas too soon to approach her. Already they had been removed to Zideon for o'er a sennight, yet not once in that time had they coupled or shared a bed. 'Twas unnatural, he conceded on a mental sigh. And what's more, 'twas like as naught destined to drive him mad.

He wanted her powerfully, he admitted as he opened his eyes, watching as Muta's blue lips took to suckling his man sac. He needed to be inside of Kara's flesh like he needed to breathe. Yet he knew not what could be done to correct the bad feelings that lay between them, feelings that were keeping them divided better than any crystal walls could ever do.

Twice he had attempted to reassure her of his emotions, to gently let her know that she had never been a mere battle prize to him, yet he knew not if his words had been believed. She had quietly thanked him, smiled softly up to him even, but then she had removed herself from the chamber without another word, lost in her own thoughts.

Cam gritted his teeth. He would give anything — everything — to be able to read his *neek'a's* mind.

The only thing that had kept him going this past sennight was the certain knowledge that her emotions were in turmoil. She might avoid him, she might even go so far as to purposely hide from him, but he knew her emotions had rarely strayed from him. He figured 'twas a promising sign for o'er the passage of time Kara K'ala Ra had learned well to school her emotions that they might not spill o'er to alert him of their existence whilst she'd been in hiding. The fact that they were now spilling o'er powerfully enough to make him aware not only of their existence but also of the fact that they were focused upon him and no other was telling unto itself.

Cam turned his head, latching his mouth around the plump nipple of a green slave who pillowed him. He sucked on the nipple, closing his eyes whilst his manhood hardened for the insatiable Muta, her lips working up and down the length of his rod once again.

He slowly fell asleep that way, much the same as he had in his youth, feeling empty inside yet knowing 'twas necessary to have his needs seen to.

His emotions were in turmoil. He could understand Kara's reasoning, goddess help him, and that meant he could understand both why she had fled in the first and why she kept herself hidden away from him even now. And yet he also knew for a certainty that he could not continue on like this.

Cam sighed. He needed his *nee'ka* in a way he'd never needed anyone or anything before.

* * * * *

Kara swam through the waters of Loch Lia-Rah with sunken hearts. Returning from the dead was overwhelming to her, she silently admitted. Every day, every hour, every moment, she was learning of new things that only served to further remind her of all the pain she had caused to her Sacred Mate by fleeing from him.

Cam's haunted eyes bespoke of torment, of pain. Even the possessions of his dominion told the same story, reflecting the fact that he had lived out five Yessat years as a man tortured. Before she had "died", Cam had christened the stronghold of planet Zideon the Palace of Dreams. When she had passed on, at least so far as he knew, he had renamed it Kopa'Ty.

A Warrior's Sorrow. Or, more simply, *My Sorrow*.

She wanted naught more than to make amends to him, to let bygones be bygones and carry on as they should have from the first, yet she feared his rejection more powerfully than ever, feared too that 'twould take a miracle from the goddess before Cam forgave her of the transgressions she'd committed against so many.

Kara closed her eyes in grief, knowing as she did that her husband must think she hated him. She could see in his eyes how much he longed for her despite everything, yet she had sent *Kefas* to his bedchamber each moon-rising rather than joining him there as she wanted to, as she should have.

She knew not why she continued to do so, except for the fact that she was afraid that after their passion had been spent together she would see naught but revulsion for her in his beautiful, haunting eyes. But she was stronger than this, she reminded herself staunchly. Leastways, if she wanted a happy life with Cam she had to at least let him know she was desirous of one.

No more bedamned pride, she vowed, as she emerged naked from the waters. She would go to him this very eve and make her charms available to him. But from there, she told

91

herself resolutely, whatever happened betwixt them was in Cam's hands.

* * * * *

Cam awoke slowly in the thick of the night, his mind groggy yet nevertheless registering the fact that he was being suckled off. He sighed, not at all in the mood to spurt for the *Kefas* yet again.

"No more," he said gruffly, his hand reaching down to thread through Muta's hair. "'Tis time for me to sleep..." His voice trailed off disbelievingly.

Cam's eyes widened and his breathing stilled when it dawned on him that the hair in his hand was not the blue hue he'd been expecting, but the black hair he'd forever dreamed of. "Kara," he rasped out, "what do you here?"

She met his eyes briefly whilst she sucked up and down the length of him, but never stopped in her ministrations long enough to answer his question. His large palm settled at the back of her head, cradling her there. "Aye," he said thickly, his breathing growing labored, "do not stop, wee one."

And she didn't. Kara closed her eyes and took him in clear to the back of her throat, working up and down the length of his cock just as her mating mistress had instructed her to do in her youth whilst she'd been bade to practice on lesser males the way of pleasing her future mate. Apparently, she thought with a secret smile, the instructions had at last paid off, for Cam was moaning and groaning, his chest heaving up and down with the effort to stop himself from spurting.

"*Nee'ka*," he rasped. "Aye. Oh aye."

When he could endure no more torture, he gently prodded her face up from his lap. She removed her lips from his cock, a suctioning sound as it popped out echoing through the bedchamber. "Ride me," he murmured, his gaze clashing with hers. "I've long dreamed of it," he thickly admitted.

Kara crawled up the long length of him, naked and as aroused as was he. She didn't make him wait, neglected even to tease him in the ways the mating mistress had suggested, for her need was as fierce as his own. "Aye," she whispered as she guided the thick head of his erection to her channel. "As have I."

On a groan, Kara sheathed his manhood within her flesh, her nipples hardening when she heard him suck in his breath. The two *Kefas* that lie abed with Cam made mewling sounds, their enchanted senses attuned to any flesh that hardened before them. Kara was more than happy to provide each one with a plump nipple to suckle, her eyes closing in bliss as the slaves further aroused her whilst she slammed her hips down upon a hungry Cam.

"I love watching slaves suckle you," he said hoarsely. "Before you fled, I looked forward to visiting with you just to see the look upon your face whilst the slaves brought you to peak after peak."

Kara's eyes narrowed in desire as she rode him harder. "I enjoyed the peaks you gave me even more," she said breathlessly.

His fingers dug into the flesh of her hips. His jaw clenched in pleasure. "As did I, *pani.*"

And then they spoke no more, for they were busy with the pleasure of mating each other hard. Kara moaned and groaned as her hips slammed down upon him, the feel of his stiff cock buried within her causing her to peak o'er and o'er again. The *Kefas* continued to suck on her nipples, their throats emitting mewling sounds each time her nipples grew harder and more elongated within their mouths.

"Come for me again," Cam ground out, his thumb massaging her clit whilst she rode him. "Let me feel that sweet pussy—oh aye," he praised her thickly, "just like that, wee one."

"*Cam.*"

Kara moaned long and loud as she bounced atop him, her flesh contracting around his whilst she burst. "*Aye,*" she groaned, her hips slamming down to impale him within her channel again and again. "*Cam.*"

Cam's teeth gritted whilst she burst, his hands digging into the flesh of her hips to hold her steady that he might spurt his hot liquid deep within her. He groaned whilst he spewed, his muscles clenching hotly, the veins in his arms cording as he came. "Kara," he groaned. "I love you."

Kara's body stilled atop his, her eyes wide as she panted for air. "Do you say this in passion?" she asked, her voice a rasp. "Or do you say this in truth?"

He was given no time to answer, for her bridal necklace began to pulse and in the blink of an eye both were moaning and groaning as they rode out endless waves of sexual euphoria. Kara gasped at the sensation, knowing why 'twas Sacred Mates would never even consider separating once they'd been joined. 'Twas more than peak, she knew. 'Twas also the emotions that assaulted them whilst they rode out the waves together.

After long minutes had passed and she was lying securely stretched out atop Cam's chest, Kara heard his voice whisper down to her. "In truth do I love you. In truth, I have always loved you."

She closed her eyes whilst she steadied herself, having been raised to believe as all Trystonni were that tears were inferior to stoicism. "Can you forgive me?" she asked quietly, hopefully.

Cam stroked her hair behind her ear. "Only if you will forgive me, *nee'ka.*"

Kara raised her head, unable to suppress the single tear that misted in her eye. "I love you too, Cam. I've always loved you."

He smiled, his eyes finding hers. "I think," he said softly, "'tis time to change the name of this palace once more."

"Aye," she agreed, her head coming down to rest o'er his hearts. She hugged him tightly. "Naught shall come between us again."

She smiled into the night, a blue moonbeam shining through the bedchamber window as they both fell into a happy, contented slumber.

Chapter Ten

Planet Khan-Gor, "Planet of the Predators"

Zyrus Galaxy, Seventh Dimension

Jana gritted her teeth as the last of her *zoka* was ripped from her body and thrown to the ground. "What are you doing?" she sputtered, whirling around to face Yorin. Her nostrils flared. "Why did—oh goddess."

Jana gasped as she watched the pupils of Yorin's eyes light up a frightening red. She took two steps away from him, backing up instinctively as she watched lasers shoot out from his eyes and singe the material of the flimsy *zoka* until naught remained of it. Her eyes wide with terror, she continued backing up, her mind desperately racing through different scenarios of escape.

Yorin's nostrils flared. "Do not back away from me, *zya*, or 'twill be another spanking for you."

Her lips curled into a snarl at the reminder of the child's punishment she'd received two moon-risings ago, the very punishment that had been doled out to her a mere Nuba-hour after she had awoken from her sennight long state of unconsciousness. Back on Galis he had vowed to punish her if she ordered him bound and tied down. He had stayed true to his word, turning her o'er his knee and spanking her bared bottom at first opportunity.

Afterwards, he had carried her to the bed of furs aboard his ship and had taken his pleasure within her flesh more times than she could count. 'Twas for a certainty she was with child. Leastways, no wench of his species could be mounted so many times without conceiving, she knew. And she indeed *was* of his species.

She knew not what had happened to her during the sennight she had been in a coma-like state, yet 'twas for a certainty that a metamorphosis of sorts had occurred within her body. Her senses were keener than once they had been, her reflexes faster, her movements more agile, and her passions more pronounced. The need to couple overcame her every other hour, and the automatic compulsion to obey him in all things forever drove her to do his bidding. 'Twas driving her mad — all of it.

Jana ignored his not so subtle threat and concentrated instead on the injustice that had been done to her. "I want to return to Galis anon," she hissed. Her eyes narrowed. "And I want the *zoka* you ruined replaced with your own credits. 'Twas an expensive material possession you just charred as naught but waste."

Yorin raised a dark brow. "You will not speak to me in such a tone, *vorah*." He gentled his voice a tad so as not to frighten her further. "And what's more, there is no such thing as credits on Khan-Gor."

She harrumphed. "Why does this knowledge not surprise me?" she asked bitterly. "You are naught but Barbarians, the lot of you." She crossed her arms under her breasts and rubbed briskly at her lower arms. 'Twas cold indeed on this primitive planet of silver ice.

"What know you of my species to make such a judgment?" he murmured.

Her nostrils flared. "I know that you have kidnapped me against my will. I know that you have denied me the use of clothing though 'tis cold enough out here to kill me. And you just admitted you've no bartering system here which can only mean you have naught worthy of bartering for."

His sharp silver eyes raked o'er her naked body. "I never said we've no bartering system," he replied absently, his mind focused on his arousal. "I only said that we do not barter with credits."

She was intrigued despite herself. She didn't want to express any interest o'er his planet in the slightest, yet her curious nature won out. "What do you barter with then?" she mumbled.

Yorin walked a step closer to her, separating the distance between them that quickly. "We barter with *yenni*."

Her eyes narrowed uncomprehendingly. "*Yenni*?" she asked incredulously. "What in the sands are those?"

His eyes flicked toward the entrance of the silver, ice-coated cave that was his lair. "Let us go inside and I will show you. 'Tis past time to feed them anyway."

Jana's eyes darted from the cave back to Yorin. "Your species barter with living creatures?"

"Aye."

She sighed, thinking that was the strangest custom she'd ever heard tell of. Waving away the enigma of the *yenni* for the moment, she returned to her earlier demand. She had no desire to enter that cave with him, but she also realized that she had no choice—for now. Eventually she would escape him and all this nonsense would be naught but a dream, but for the interim she could only bide her time. "If you want me to accompany you inside of my own will, then 'tis for a certainty," she said staunchly, "that you will clothe me." Her hand swept about in a manner meant to broach no argument. "'Tis nigh unto chilling out here. 'Twill be a thousand times colder within a dark cave."

Yorin's lips curled into a half-smile. "'Tis not exceedingly cold within our lair, *vorah*. Nor is it dark. 'Tis lit of gel-fire."

By this point in the conversation, Jana's teeth were chattering from the frigid temperature of Khan-Gor. Her bared feet were freezing, standing upon the silver ice ground as she was. Every second they remained without grew worse. "Why d-do you not c-clothe me?" she asked again, for some perverse reason wanting to hear the real answer.

His gaze devoured her naked body as the thumb and index finger of one of his hands reached toward a nipple and rolled it around between them. She sucked in her breath, immediately aroused.

"Because," he murmured, his predator eyes narrowing in possessiveness, "males of my species do not take chances with their mates."

Jana's breathing stilled as she considered the significance of his words. She feared she already understood his meaning, but asked the question anyway. "What d-do y-you mean?" she chattered out.

Yorin plucked her up off of the icy ground, no longer willing to abide her foolishness. She would catch her death if she continued to stand out here in the cold. Cradling her close to his body, he swaddled her within the warmth of the animal pelt he was wearing, then made for his lair.

"I mean," he explained in an implacable tone of voice as he strode toward the entrance to the cave, "that males of my species allow their mates no clothing because 'tis impossible to flee from us whilst naked."

Jana bit down on her lip to keep from whimpering aloud. He was telling the truth and she knew it. In an icy climate such as this one, a wench on the run from the male who'd claimed her would last mayhap a Nuba-hour before expiring without clothing to warm her.

If she was considering ways she might thieve animal pelts from Yorin, she kept her thoughts to herself.

* * * * *

Piloting through the black depths of deep space, Kari Gy'at Li glanced over to where Dari sat beside her. The princess was silent, her eyes narrowed in thought as she stared out of the gastrolight cruiser's wide porthole.

It had been a long day, an even longer week, Kari thought wearily. They had followed the trail dictated to them by Talia, the Chief High Mystik of Galis, yet so far they had learned very little in the way of useful information.

They still didn't know where the Evil One had originated from, nor did they even know who or what it really was. All that they knew was that the information was out there— somewhere—and that they needed to find it before the Evil One found them.

"Where should we go now?" Kari asked softly, turning back to face the vastness of space.

Dari sighed as she tiredly smoothed back a few strands of micro-braids. "I think you should pilot us to the far reaches of this galaxy, just to see if what we learned on the last planet has any truth to it at all."

Kari snorted at that. "I doubt it. As exploratory a people as the citizens of Trek Mi Q'an are, surely somebody would have discovered this ice planet if indeed it truly exists." She shook her head. "Those males on planet Brekkon didn't look to be the most reputable or reliable of sources."

Dari tried to smile at her words, but found the movement too taxing. "Have you a better idea then?" she challenged.

"No." Kari sighed. "Unfortunately I don't."

"Then what harm will it do us to at least go see for ourselves?"

"Point taken."

Neither woman said anything more on the subject as Kari Gy'at Li steered the gastrolight cruiser toward an encroaching wormhole. But then there wasn't much that could be said. They could either check out every possibility no matter how small, or they could surrender themselves in defeat and be killed off in the process.

By now the Evil One surely knew that Dari and Bazi had escaped. 'Twas only a matter of time until it came looking for them...and mayhap found them.

* * * * *

"This," Jana squeaked, "are *yenni*?" She stared unblinking down at the creatures, unable to believe what it was she was seeing. They hadn't even reached the lair proper yet, she thought apprehensively, and already, only three feet inside the cave's entrance, they'd come upon these...pets. What in the sands else would she find here?

"Aye," Yorin absently answered her as he removed the animal pelt that had covered his upper body, exposing his massively muscled arms and chest. His lips curved into a frown. "It looks as though they haven't been fed in days," he said angrily. "My brothers know better than to go off without one of them remaining behind to feed them."

When Yorin began removing the animal skin kilt-like covering that he wore, Jana's jaw dropped open. "How do you plan to feed them?" she sputtered.

His eyebrows rose fractionally at her reaction, but he said naught to chastise her. 'Twas all new to her, he realized. Given time she would accept the ways of Khan-Gor as her own. "With seed, of course."

Jana thought 'twas possible her jaw was hanging open wide enough for it to touch the ground. "Life-force?" she squeaked. "The staple of their diet is life-force?"

"Aye." Naked, he strode toward the pen, stopping only briefly to apologize. He combed his fingers gently through her hair. "'Twas not my intention to take the time to feed them on the very moon-rising I brought you home, yet 'tis apparent

101

from the fact that these creatures of the night are sleeping whilst 'tis dark that they are lethargic from lack of food."

Jana's teeth clicked shut. She could only stare at him dumbly.

"Go on and explore your new home, *vorah*," he said on a nod. "'Twill like as naught take me a couple of hours before they've had their fill."

She returned his nod, yet never moved from her position. Too curious to leave just yet if at all, she watched in fascination as Yorin entered the pen and walked towards a bed of soft animal pelts.

Tethered by golden choke collars that were secured to the wall of the cave by long leashes, were a pack of creatures that looked much like humanoid wenches save for their luminescent white skins and sharp, icy looking tails. And, of course, the fact that they preferred moving about on all fours to standing upright.

Otherwise, however, the *yenni* looked remarkably like humanoid wenches. They sported large, full breasts, puffy labias that looked ripe and ready for a male's thrusting, as well as beautiful faces. If the staple of their diet was Kahn-Gor male life-force, 'twas obvious now to Jana why these creatures were used for bartering. Much like *Kefas*, they were insatiable pleasure-givers. And just as the *Kefas* had no thought processes, the *yenni* too looked to harbor none either. Leastways, if they were possessed of thought processes, 'twas the simplistic reasoning of lower animals, their main goal in life to stay well-fed.

If Jana had thought the creatures were too similar to humanoid wenches for her to have a care for, such doubt was laid to rest when she saw the first *yenni* take notice of Yorin's presence and bound o'er to him. She leapt on all fours in a lightning-fast movement, her tail whipping about excitedly at the realization that she was nigh close to being fed. A scarce second later the rest of the pack took notice of the master and in the blink of an eye, they had tackled him in their excitement, causing him to land upon the bedding with a thump.

Yorin laughed as he landed on his backside, then groaned when the dominant female of the group popped her suctioning lips around his cock.

Yet another difference from humanoid wenches, Jana noted with interest. The lips of the *yenni* were exceedingly puffy when wrapped around a cock, as if they had been made to suckle males dry.

She sighed. By the holy sands of Tryston, why had she ever left Ti Q'won? Had she not fled, she wearily conceded, then she never would have went to Galis. And had she never ventured into Galis, then she never would have been kidnapped by Yorin only to end up here watching this bizarre event unfold.

Jana took a deep breath as she absently smoothed a tendril of golden hair back from her brow line. She was tired. Cold and tired. 'Twas not so cold as it had been outside of the cave, but 'twas still chilly enough to keep her nipples hard and goose bumps dotting her skin.

She was confused. For two moon-risings now she had been awake and at Yorin's side, yet she still didn't understand why 'twas she had been taken by him in the first. Nor did she understand what he had been doing on Galis, or how he had ended up within Klykka's harem. When she had put her bevy of questions to the giant predator, he had but smiled in that aggravating way of his, then murmured that all would be revealed to her when at last they'd reached his lair on Khan-Gor.

Well, she thought tiredly, they were on Khan-Gor and strictly speaking within his lair, yet still she had no answers. And, she thought on a sigh, judging by the ferocious cock suckling Yorin was receiving just now, she doubted anything in the way of enlightenment would be hers anytime soon.

Jana's eyes flicked down the rocky path that led to the lair proper. She bit her lip, wondering if she should go inside without Yorin that she might rest for a spell. She was exhausted. So bedamned bone-weary and —

"Mmm, aye."

Yorin's dreamily uttered words induced her head to pivot back around to watch him as he fed the *yenni*. His eyes were closed in bliss, his cock poking straight upwards as it disappeared within the dominant female's mouth. Since Jana had already heard him spurt twice, she knew 'twas a third feeding for the dominant female. She could only speculate how many spurts 'twould take before she was filled.

Having been raised on a planet where males kept harems until they were mated, and indeed kept *Kefas* even after they'd been mated, Jana felt no pangs of jealousy whilst watching the feeding take place. Instead she felt mere curiosity, for she'd never heard tell of natural creatures that needed seed to exist. And, if she were honest with herself, she also felt arousal coalescing and cording within her, for the sound of so much purring whilst the females of the pack licked all o'er Yorin's body was unexpectedly provocative.

The *yenni* licked him everywhere, the saltiness of his skin apparently a treat of sorts to them as well. Whilst the dominant female continued to feed, her suctioning lips working up and down his thick cock in a frenzied manner that induced Yorin to moan and groan, the beta females lapped at every other part of his body, their tongues sucking salt from his neck, his nipples, his man sac, even his knees and toes.

The look on Yorin's face was one of carnal bliss mixed with pain. He kept moaning and groaning, then, his eyes shut tightly, eventually began crying out in sounds that were nigh unto tortured.

Jana winced, wondering to herself if the females were harming him, then walked closer to the pen to see what 'twas they were about. Her eyes widened.

Yorin was definitely not being tortured. In fact, just the opposite. The reason the giant Barbarian was crying out so loudly was because the dominant female was allowing him no surcease. She suckled upon his cock frenziedly, wildly, in a manner that 'twould cause any male to spurt hard and long, yet she kept him from bursting by gripping his man sac in her hands and gently tugging it away from his body.

The dominant female knew how to feed, Jana thought as her arousal grew more pronounced. The lead *yenni* was forcing Yorin's man sac to jam up with seed that when she released it and allowed the tight sac to hit his body, his spurt would be violently hard.

Jana watched in fascination as the *yenni* continued to suckle him, one of her hands still firmly latched around his man sac, her suctioning lips working up and down his shaft with incredible speed. Yorin moaned and groaned, his head flailing about wildly, his man sac turning from a bronzed color to a bluish one.

"Feed from me," Yorin commanded the female in the Khan-Gori tongue. His nostrils flared as his chest heaved up and down. "Drink of me anon!" he bellowed.

On a mewling sound that further reminded Jana of *Kefa* slaves, the dominant female obeyed, releasing his man sac and allowing it to flick back at his body. Yorin growled as he burst, fangs exploding into his mouth, his eyes lighting a primitive red, as he spurted a ferociously hard load of seed into the female's awaiting mouth.

His chest continued to heave up and down as he patted the *yenni* atop the head. "Good girl," he murmured as she lapped up all the seed there was to be had from his spurt. "Now go lie down and let the others feed." When a mew of protest issued from her throat, Yorin gave up on a sigh. "You must be nigh unto starving." He laid back and allowed her to continue, his eyes closing once more as the process began anew, repeating itself for the fourth time.

Minutes later, after four wicked helpings, the dominant female moved away from Yorin and strolled lazily on all fours to the other side of the pen that she might sleep. Jana could tell she was well sated, for a contented purring sound rumbled low in her chest as she licked at herself before falling into a deep sleep.

Now 'twas the turn of the others and each of the *yenni* saw to it that they got their fill of Khan-Gori seed. Jana knew not how much time had gone by when at last the final female moved away from him, contentedly purring as she crept to where she would sleep, but she knew it had been hours. By the time the feeding was done, Jana had been worked up into a state of need that could rival any *yenni's* hunger.

Yorin's eyes raked o'er her, the need within them apparent. "Come here, *zya*," he said thickly. "I've the need of your flesh...and blood."

Jana's breathing grew labored, sporadic. Ever since she had awoken from her metamorphosis, the need to couple came upon her urgently and regularly. She had been denied the impaling she needed whilst Yorin had fed the *yenni*, and now her body wanted that fact remedied. She closed her eyes, wondering for the hundredth time what had become of her.

"Come," he murmured. "I'm stiff for need of you."

"How can you be stiff," she gasped, arousal hitting her hard, "when you have spurted no fewer than twenty times to feed your pets?" Her eyes opened slowly, and she saw the proof of his words for herself. He looked so wicked, she thought, so powerful and masculine as he laid there amongst the animal pelts, his cock poking upward, drunk on his own arousal. "'Tis unfathomable," she muttered.

One black eyebrow rose. "Is it?" he asked softly. His silver eyes narrowed in lust as they ran o'er her. "Do you not remember," he said thickly, "what it feels like when we mate...what it feels like when we drink of each other whilst we are both spurting?"

Jana's breasts heaved up and down as she tried in vain to stifle her body's reaction to him and his words. Oh aye, she remembered. She remembered too well.

"Twenty spurts into the mouths of starving *yenni*," he rasped out, "cannot hope to compare to even a single spurt within your milking cunt, *zya*."

Sweat broke out onto her brow. Her breasts heaved violently. Her clit swelled and pulsed with the need to couple.

"Come to me, *vorah*." *Come to me, wife.*

Fangs exploded into her mouth. A growl erupted from her throat. In an animalistic instinct that seemed almost second nature, Jana flung herself o'er the wall of the pen in one far-reaching leap, then came down upon him and impaled her flesh with his cock in one fluid motion.

She fucked him hard and primally, inducing him to bellow and growl. Her breasts jiggled up and down as she milked moan after moan out of him, then his hands reached out to cup them that he might massage her nipples as he was wont to do.

Jana's hips slammed down upon him as she frenziedly fucked him, her flesh wanting his seed. The sound of blood pulsing through his jugular vein unleashed a knot of arousal in her belly, and on a growl, she burst and exploded around him.

Yorin groaned as her fangs tore through his neck and suckled of his warm, fresh essence. He was so delirious with pleasure that his eyes rolled back into his head. As she fed of him, as she continued suckling at his ripest vein, his fingers dug into the flesh of her hips and aided her body in slamming down upon his, his cock ramming and cramming further and further into her suctioning pussy with each thrust.

She never once released his jugular whilst she rode him, and Yorin thought 'twould drive him mad with arousal. Her wee six-foot frame stretched out upon his like a doll's, her face buried against his neck, her hips frantically slamming downwards, all of it instinctually done in the need of finding surcease.

"Aye," he gritted out, his orgasm fast approaching, "you've the juiciest cunt in all the galaxies, wee *vorah*."

And then he was spurting within her, a growl of completion torn from his throat as his man sac burst of seed. In a matter of seconds, his fangs were tearing into the flesh of her neck and he frenziedly sipped of her whilst she screamed in maddening pleasure atop him.

Yorin rolled her to her back and fucked her flesh long and primitively. He mated her hard, rode her body to peak countless times, pounded in and out of her until she'd milked his cock thrice more.

When 'twas done, when he'd mated her to satiation, he rolled o'er once more and bade her to sleep upon his belly. She purred contentedly atop him, her much smaller stature intimately snuggled against him.

From where she lay atop him, her fangs at last retreating into her gums, Jana fell asleep feeling loved and secure in a way so powerful 'twas for a certainty she had never before experienced it. And yet as she stretched and yawned, she couldn't help but to wonder what other Khan-Gori surprises lay in wait for her, what other astonishing things would be thrust upon her.

Instinctually, and unable to resist, Jana's tongue darted out and curled around Yorin's flat male nipple, suckling the salt from his skin. She was no better than a *yenni*, she thought with a pang of fright, for there was naught in this world or any other that could keep her from milking him of seed, or from lapping away the salt upon his sweat-soaked skin.

She fell asleep thinking about Yorin's lair, apprehensively wondering what she would find within it.

Chapter Eleven

Meanwhile, back on Zideon...

Kara's eyes filled with tears as her sire swung her up into his arms and hugged her as though he never wanted to let go. She wept openly, allowing her hot tears to track down her cheeks unchecked, wetting them both.

She had expected to feel overwhelmed with joy upon seeing her *mani* and sire again, yet nothing could have prepared her for the surge of emotion she had felt when first she had embraced her *mani*, and now as she was held by her papa. After all that she had done to hurt them, after allowing them to believe her dead for five Yessat years, they were both accepting her back into their lives with open arms—and without recrimination.

In truth, Kara wished that they would yell at her, that they would accuse her of all that she was guilty of, for 'twould do much to ease her plaguing guilt. Instead, she was being showered with naught but love of the hearts and genuine gratitude of the fact that their beloved daughter had at last returned home. 'Twas wondrous indeed, yet 'twas for a certainty that she felt she didn't deserve it.

"Ah goddess, my hearts," Zor whispered into her hair. "You have been sorely missed, wee one."

Kara smiled through her tears, hugging her sire tightly. "As have you," she choked out. "There were many moon-risings throughout the years that I longed to come home, yet I feared 'twould be no welcome for me there."

"How could you think that?" he rasped out. "'Tis naught I wouldn't have given to have you safely back."

Kara held onto his neck tightly, having missed him so much. She could feel Cam's eyes upon her, so she raised her face from her sire's shoulder and gazed at him through teary lashes. He winked, a silent communication reminding her that he had been right and that her parents had wanted her back regardless to everything. She smiled at him softly, telling him without words how much she loved him, how much she would always love him.

"I'm telling you sweetheart," Kyra said shakily as Zor set their daughter back down on her feet that his *nee'ka* might embrace their hatchling again, "if you ever pull any dumb stunts like that again I'll…"

"Oh goddess, *mani*," Kara said on a groan. "Think you I could ever bear to be separated from Cam, papa, and you again?"

"The answer had better be no," she sniffed, reaching out to run her fingers through her daughter's hair. "My heart couldn't handle it."

"Nor could mine," Cam murmured as he walked up to join the hugging, teary-eyed trio. He put his arm around his *nee'ka* and squeezed her gently. "Mayhap now you understand why 'tis important you tell us all that you know in regards to Dari and Jana's whereabouts." He bent down and kissed her atop the head. "Just as your parents grieved o'er you, so too do Queen Geris and King Dak grieve the loss of their hatchlings."

Kara shook her head. "'Twas truth I told you, husband. Verily, I know not where they have gone." She sighed, her expression growing troubled. "Though in truth I fear the worst. Jana and I have always been best friends. If 'twas possible for her to contact me…"

"Then she would have done so," Kyra murmured. She took a deep breath and gazed up at her husband. "I hope Dak finds them—both of them. I have a bad feeling about…something I can't quite put my finger on," she muttered.

"As do I." Zor's look was thoughtful as he gazed down at his daughter. "In truth, my hearts, I am fair bursting with questions to put to you about the years you spent removed from us. And yet—" He waved toward the raised table within the palace's great hall. "—'tis mayhap best if I save those questions for later that we might discuss Jana and Dari anon."

Cam nodded. "Gio and Death have sent word of their imminent arrival. They wish to put questions to my *nee'ka* as well."

Kara sighed, but nodded. "I will be what help I can be, Cam, yet I truly do not—"

"I know," he said softly, his turquoise eyes glowing lovingly. "I believe you when you say you've no notion where they've gone."

Kara smiled, secure in the knowledge that the deuce of them would never again lack for faith and trust in the other. "I'll see what I can do," she murmured.

* * * * *

The desperateness Gio felt to reach Dari was so tangible as to make Kara feel a pity for him. She closed her eyes briefly, reminded anew of the grief Cam must have felt whilst she'd been removed to Galis.

"I must," Gio rasped out from his bench at the raised table, "have Dari back anon." His mind raced with memories of the male that had called to her aboard the gastrolight cruiser. 'Twas enough to make his stomach knot up and feel sickened. "For a certainty," he continued on, "you must know something—anything—I could find useful."

"And I must find the fiery-headed wench who accompanies her," Death rumbled out. He ran a strong hand o'er his jaw. "'Tis of dire consequence that I find her."

Kyra's brow furrowed. "Fiery-headed?" she asked. Her eyes narrowed thoughtfully. On earth, the color of her hair had been considered rare. In Trek Mi Q'an, it was a downright anomaly.

Kara nodded. "'Twas much the same as yours, *mani*," she confirmed. "In fact, she looked so much like you I found it eerie at times." She smiled, remembering the woman who had cared for her, who had helped her grow into a strong wench. "Leastways, Kari Gy'at Li never spoke much of her past, though I know she heralded from a place outside the seventh dimension."

Kyra's heart began to race. She felt chills racing up and down her spine. It couldn't be...could it? "How strongly did she resemble me? Was her accent similar to mine?"

"Aye." Kara's gaze drank in her mother's. "'Twas one in the same." Her eyes narrowed thoughtfully. "I wish I could tell you more, truly I do, but Kari Gy'at Li never spoke of her former life. 'Twas as if..."

"What?" Kyra asked quietly. She leaned in closer to her daughter. "It was as if what?"

Kara sighed, not quite able to eloquently express the gut feeling she'd long harbored in respect to Kari. "'Twas as if she felt too haunted by memories to think back on her past," she murmured. "I think she mayhap lost someone who was quite special to her before she landed in Galis."

Kyra bit her lip, her eyes falling to the crystal tabletop. "I see." Silence permeated the chamber for a lingering moment, until the Empress' head shot up and her gaze clashed with her daughter's. "Do you have any holo-images of her, sweetheart?"

Kara's brow furrowed. "Why is this so important to you, *mani*?"

"Please," Kyra said shakily. "Go fetch the holo-image, honey."

Cam waved his hand at a bound servant, instructing her when she approached him that she should go upstairs and fetch a particular piece of his *nee'ka's* jewelry. When he had snatched her away from Galis, 'twas one of the few possessions she'd been wearing at the time.

When the servant had gone, Gio turned to Kara once more. His jaw was clenched, his expression tight. "Mayhap Dari mentioned to you where 'twas she wished to experience a time of freedom." He spread his hands. "Any information, no matter how trivial you think it, would be of use to me."

Kara blinked, having forgotten that train of thought for a spell. "A time of freedom?" she asked, not following.

"Aye. 'Tis the reason she left me, just as you left Cam."

Kara blushed at the reminder. There had been more to it than freedom on her part, but the reasons were complex and private. But then, so too were Dari's. She decided then and there that she would tell him what little she knew about Dari's troubles without making references to Bazi. Dari had convinced her 'twas important none knew he accompanied her. "I do not think she fled Arak for freedom, Gio, but because she feared for her safety there."

Gio's gaze narrowed. "She told you I did not care for her well?" he asked icily.

"Nay. Nay! 'Twas not you..."

His eyes narrowed uncomprehendingly.

"In truth," Kara whispered, "she did fear for *your* safety more than her own." She knew 'twas mayhap more than she should have said, but with each passing moment, her fear for Dari and Kari grew more acute. She knew not the why of it, only that she felt thusly.

Zor grunted. "Why in the sands would she fear for Gio's safety? That makes no sense, my hearts."

"Aye," Gio rasped out. "I can see it in your eyes that you are hiding something from us. Please tell me."

Kara bit her lip, but said nothing.

"*Pani*," Cam said softly, "if you know aught, 'tis best do you tell it. Leastways, you would never forgive yourself did Dari meet a bad end."

Kara could feel the eyes of everyone upon her and the effect was nigh unto unnerving. Could she betray a confidence, especially when Dari had kept her and Jana's secret for five Yessat years? But then again, could she continue to ignore the nagging premonition that told her 'twas a matter of life and death that Gio find her younger cousin?

"In truth, Dari told me very little," Kara admitted. "She has ever been the type to hold her own council."

Gio nodded, realizing as much.

"But five years ago when first Jana and I fled..."

"Aye," Zor prodded her, "go on."

Kara sighed. "Dari was supposed to accompany us." She ignored everyone's wide-eyed expressions and plowed on. "Jana and I were to dock at the holo-port in Trader City on Arak and await her there. But before we could land, she sent out a holo-call, instructing us to venture onward to Galis because she could not yet leave Arak."

"Why?" Gio asked, his hearts rate speeding up at the knowledge that he had nigh unto lost her once before without even knowing it. "Why did she wish to remain behind?"

Kara shrugged helplessly. "I do not know. Leastways, she hadn't much time and kept looking o'er her shoulder as though she feared she'd been followed. But," she said in a whisper of a voice, "she did say something, and 'twas something that ever haunted Jana and I until at last we were reunited with her again."

"What did she say?" Gio murmured.

"She said there was an evil on Arak," Kara said unblinkingly. "An evil that needed to be destroyed before it destroyed her...and you."

Death's body stilled. Every muscle in his large body corded and tensed. "An evil?" he repeated, needing confirmation.

"Aye." Kara shook her head, her expression sad. "Yet she would never confess to me what this evil was, not even when we were reunited with her on Galis. She kept insisting 'twas best if we remained unawares."

Gio was torn between elation that Dari hadn't left him for naught but freedom after all, fear that his betrothed was embroiled in a dangerous situation he wasn't there to aid her of, and a desperate need to find her. Memories of that bedamned male's voice besieged him.

From beside him, Death's mind was reeling, his desperation to reach Kari bordering on fear. Fear that if he didn't capture her anon, something else would. And yet, he said naught of what he knew. He understood now why Dari had held her tongue so many years.

"Dari ventured into Valor City with Kari to seek information she might use to her advantage against this evil." Kara shrugged her shoulders. "I know naught what she learned from the Chief High Mystik there for 'twas the same moon-rising Cam found me."

Gio and Death shot up from their seats, both of them feeling hopeful for the first time. If there was any information at all to be gleaned in Valor City, they would ferret it out for a certainty.

Gio stopped briefly on his way out to place a hand upon Kara's shoulder. "Thank you," he said quietly. And with that, he departed the palace.

Kara took a deep breath as she looked at Cam. She knew they were both hoping Dari and Jana were found alive and well. And Kari. Kara had lived but five years with the fiery wench, yet she had been like a second *mani* to her.

Just then the bound servant returned, her naked breasts bobbing up and down as she made her way to the raised table. She handed the piece of jewelry to Kara, then quietly left for the kitchens.

"Ah here we go," Kara said to her *mani*. "Now let me find the holo-image of Kari Gy'at Li for you."

Kyra nodded, her eyes widening. She nibbled on her lip, desperate to see it.

Zor studied his wife inquiringly. "Is aught wrong, my hearts?"

"I don't know," Kyra said simply, leaving her answer at that.

Kara flicked through the images that popped out of the small charm that had dangled from the chain about her ankle the moon-rising she'd been captured by Cam. "'Tis not here," she grumbled, flicking rapidly o'er the holo-images again. "I scarce believe it."

"Damn it," Kyra muttered, her eyes narrowed in thought.

"*Nee'ka?*" Zor said softly. "What is wrong?"

Kyra glanced up at him, distracted. She sighed. "Nothing," she said softly, looking away. "I was just being a damn fool."

* * * * *

"I love you, *pani*." Cam kissed Kara's temple, his hands stroking lazily o'er the flesh of her buttocks. They had finished making love but moments ago, yet the need for her closeness was upon him as greatly as ever.

"I love you too." Kara raised her head to look at him, her Q'ana Tal glowing blue eyes shimmering. "I've always loved you. You know that in your hearts now, do you not?"

"Aye." He grinned. "I know it."

She placed a quick kiss on his chest then raised her face to his once more. "And I know now that you've always loved me. We will never be apart from the other again."

"'Tis a vow amongst Sacred Mates," he murmured.

"'Tis a vow amongst Sacred Mates," she repeated.

In a lightening-quick movement, Cam rolled her to her back and entered her wet channel with a long thrust. He groaned at the pleasure, greedily wanting to stay within her as he'd dreamed every moon-rising of doing before he'd had the right of it by the Holy Law. He had spent the longest part of his life awaiting the moon-rising when she would at last be his. Now he finally had her. 'Twould ever be this way.

"Let me watch whilst a *Kefa* pleasures you," he rasped out. "Let me carry you to our bathing hole, *pani*."

Kara wrapped her long legs around his middle. "You were ever the wily one, husband."

He grinned as he bent his neck to kiss her. "Aye. Some things never change."

Epilogue

Naked under the stolen animal pelts she wore, Jana's breasts bobbed up and down as she wound her way through the rocky, iced terrain of the cold silver landscape. 'Twas nigh unto impossible to see where she was going with the night so black upon this planet, yet she had been given no choice but to wait for Yorin to fall in his slumber before attempting to escape him.

And escape him she would.

The things that she had been made to endure—how could any wench humbly submit to them? She ignored the shamefully brazen voice that declared she'd not only endured them, but had in fact enjoyed them, and sprinted at a speed no wench of her species could have moved without having undergone a metamorphosis to make it possible.

She wanted her *mani* and papa, she thought wildly. She cared not of any recriminations that might stem from having fled all those years back. She would gladly take any of them did it mean she would feel her *mani's* hand upon her brow once again, or feel her sire's arms clasped about her.

Jana cried out in mental anguish, wondering if 'twas possible they might reject her when they learned of the species she had become. She was no longer like a Trystonni, she thought in horror. She could do—things. Bizarre, frightening things. And the way she drank of Yorin whilst they mated—good goddess it didn't bear dwelling o'er.

She put her bad thoughts from her mind, concentrating once again on the mission at hand. She had to escape. 'Twas now or 'twas never. She had done the unthinkable and thwarted the warriors of Tryston once before. So too could she thwart the Khan-Goris, making them believe she'd died.

Jana was sharp enough to realize that her only hope of successfully fleeing her mate was in finding a holo-port that would transport her to her own galaxy. She refused to consider the fact that in her sennight on Khan-Gor, she had seen not even one holo-port dotting the landscape.

Yorin had firmly told her that there was no sense in running from him for 'twas impossible to leave Khan-Gor without a ship, yet she refused to give up hope that mayhap he had lied to her. Even if he had been telling her naught but truths, she was a warrior woman now, and a warrior woman would simply find another method of escape.

Jana's nostrils flared, her will growing stronger by the Nuba-second. And yet, she admitted, she could scarce contain the little girl words that kept swimming through her mind:

Papa, she thought desperately, sending out the fiercest wave of emotion she had purposely emitted in years, please come for me…

* * * * *

"My God," Kari breathed out, her silver-blue eyes wide. "I don't believe it. The Brekkons were correct."

"Aye," Dari murmured, her eyes seeking out Bazi's. "Khan-Gor is real."

Bazi took a deep breath, then nodded. "What will we do now?"

The women gazed out the wide porthole, their eyes taking in the sight of the large silver-ice planet none in Trek Mi Q'an had even known existed. 'Twas unbelievable. And if the Brekkons had been correct on this score, mayhap their legends of the Barbarians who dwelled here had a basis in truth as well.

119

"We will land," Kari decided, realizing as she did that they had come too far to back off now.

Dari nodded. "And we will find the key." She sighed, looking back at Bazi. "Mayhap then we can destroy the Evil One," she murmured.

His young eyes were troubled. "Are you certain you wish to do this?" he asked quietly. "Mayhap it should be me who does it alone."

"Nay," Dari said firmly. "We made vows unto the other. Leastways," she insisted, "I would sooner throw myself into a nest of *heeka-beasts* than not see this through to its fruition."

"But he will never forgive you," Bazi said quietly, guilt lancing through him. "Your betrothed will never forgive—"

"I know," Dari said softly. She sighed, her eyes flicking back toward the primitive planet coated in ice. "I can never again return to Gio." She closed her eyes. "He will never forgive me for murdering his own sire."

* * * * *

Her thoughts a million miles away, her memories filled with the days so many hundreds of years ago when she'd lived on earth, Kyra swore under her breath when she lost her footing and tripped over—she didn't know what.

"Damn it," she muttered, crouching down to pick up a charm that had fallen from her daughter's anklet. "I am having one hell of a bad—"

Her eyes widened when it dawned on her that the charm no doubt contained holo-images within it as most anklet charms did. She clutched the crystal charm to her breasts, her breathing growing labored as she stood up. "Maybe this charm holds the holo-image Kara lost," she said shakily.

She didn't know why she was breathing so heavily, or why sweat had broken out all over her body. But she felt desperate to open the charm, to view whatever images lay in waiting within the piece of crystal jewelry. She fiddled with the unlocking mechanism, cursing when it didn't immediately pop open.

"Damn it!" she swore, her nostrils flaring as she continued to fiddle with it. "Why won't this thing...open," she finished softly.

When the charm gave way, when the holo-images displayed before her, her hand flew up to cover her mouth. She backed into a wall, her eyes filling with tears, as the image of a red-headed woman who could have been her twin shimmered then appeared before her.

"Oh my God," Kyra breathed out, chills racing up and down her spine. "Oh my God."

To Be Continued...

"Naughty Nancy" in Strictly Taboo: Book 4.5, Installment 5

and

NO FEAR

Book 5, Installment 6

Made in the USA
Middletown, DE
01 April 2019